Please return this book on or before the date marked above. If over-
due a charge will be made in accordance with library regulations.

The period of loan may be extended (once only by post or tele-
phone) if the book is not required by another reader. To renew,
please quote either YOUR TICKET NUMBER (at computerised
libraries), or AUTHOR, TITLE, DATE DUE and

▼ ——— THIS NUMBER ——— ▼

181
148

Seasons of the Gun

Duty had brought Duane Everson from the warm south back to cold Montana where he'd never expected an arrogant father and suspicious siblings to make his homecoming anything but tough. But the reality was worse than he could ever have imagined, for evil was abroad in the high country.

When the blood began to spill and the lawless slipped their leashes, the gentle spring and summer of Chain Range, Cloud Valley Ranch and Red Warrior River were brutally transformed into the seasons of the gun.

By the same author:

Branded
Where Legends Ride

Seasons of the Gun

Paul Wheelahan

A Black Horse Western

ROBERT HALE · LONDON

© Paul Wheelahan 2001
First published in Great Britain 2001

ISBN 0 7090 6910 3

Robert Hale Limited
Clerkenwell House
Clerkenwell Green
London EC1R 0HT

Typeset by
Derek Doyle & Associates, Liverpool.
Printed and bound in Great Britain by
Antony Rowe Limited, Wiltshire.

1

Goin' Home

The wind was erratic as it always was just before dawn, and the earth beneath his horse's hoofs was spongy from the rains that had overtaken him crossing Chain Range. Tilting hat-brim against the cut of the breeze, Duane was calculating exactly how much further it was along the switchbacks of this faint deer-pad down to the valley, when abruptly he drew rein to pull the black to a stop.

Lean and upright in his saddle, he sat motionless with every outdoors-honed sense working overtime. Something had come to him on this chill Montana night wind, some sound, scent or stirring that didn't hit him quite right. But what?

He waited. Patience was part of him and he knew these wilds well. Still. This section of rugged country lying south-east and below timber-rich Drumgriff Basin, and adjacent to his destination, Cloud Valley Ranch, he knew better than most, having been born and raised just a few miles from this backtrail he was travelling for the first time in eight long years.

Duane 'Rider' Everson was coming home at last. And now trail's end was so close he was impatient for warmth, food and shelter, and yes, even the inevitable confrontation with his father.

Let's keep going and get it over and done with, said his mind. But his instinct countered with caution; 'Wait until your neck hair settles a little and Joker stops toggling his ears that way he does when he's uneasy.' He shrugged beneath his slicker. It had been five weeks in the saddle since he'd set out from far Arizona, so another few minutes' delay wasn't going to make much difference now.

Spring was marching across the mountains and plains of Montana, mounting a verdant assault to win back the land. But winter was staging a rearguard action tonight, growling as it retreated into the mountain fastnesses, and his blood, thinned by the southern sun, was reminding him that eight years could be a long, long time even if you said it quick.

The cough, when it came, sounded gunshot loud to his straining ears. Somewhere ahead and below his position, maybe as close as some thirty to forty paces distant, judging by the sound, a man had cleared his throat.

It didn't figure. This game track, which switchbacked its erratic trace down off a rugged line of timbered ridges to the valley's southern pastures, was never used by the hands and only rarely by hunters. The only reason he was travelling it this raw morning was because he knew it intimately and was shaving every last horse-mile possible. Who could be up here at this time of night? Who would want to be?

Time passed. The sound was not repeated. For a moment he considered shouting to alert whoever it was he was coming through, but innate caution stayed his hand. He was a practical man of twenty-five summers who hadn't survived an action-filled life by taking chances. The practicality of his nature suggested that anybody skulking about on a goat-track trace in the dark hour before dawn on a night like this just might not be up to anything honest.

The weariness left him as he straightened his shoulders and eased the horse forward with his knees. The wind was in his face, carrying whatever sounds he might make away from that shadow-shrouded gulch where he figured his man had to be. He rode with infinite caution, a shadow blended of man, saddle and mount. He was alert yet relaxed in the saddle, his horse responding to every whisper, every pressure of hands or knees.

The shoulders of the gulch now loomed above him on either side. His listening intensified; the automatic checking of the small natural sounds, and the constant probing that sought and sorted each wind-stirred motion in the brush, searching for anything that didn't belong here and discarding those shadows which rightly belonged to the night.

So it was that he rode soundlessly to within mere feet of the blocky figure hunched miserably against a slab of granite, before the fellow realized he had company.

Cat-quick and cursing, he whirled with a curse and the grey light glinted on the rifle in his hands.

'Wha-what the hell do you think you're doin'?' he croaked, backing up and almost stumbling. 'Git them paws up, mister. Who the hell are you? C'mon, git down where I can see you, goddamnit! Move!'

The dawn light was slowly strengthening and

Duane could see the man was a stranger, certainly nobody who'd worked for his father way back when. He looked mean and dangerous and was jerking that rifle about like someone who just might use it. Maybe the smart thing to do would be to dismount as ordered. Yet he remained right where he was, hands crossed on the pommel and hat tugged low over his eyes. His very poise in the face of a threat along with the way his jaw muscles worked might have warned a more perceptive man to step wary.

For suddenly all the miles, the anxiety and the nagging uncertainty of the past weeks, came crowding in on Rider Duane. Alone and edgy, he'd traversed one fifth of the nation, putting behind him desert, mountain and plain to finally raise Cloud Valley at the fag end of twenty-four hours straight in the saddle, only to be challenged by a stranger with a gun a bare half-mile from home. He might well be prepared for a confrontation with his father, but he wasn't taking this.

'Get down or I'll blast you, so help me God—'

That was as far as the gunman got. The light pressure of Duane's right boot-toe against the black's brisket was a familiar signal to the best working horse on Alameda Ranch. It meant go forward hard, no matter what. Mostly the signal was given when the rider wanted some unbroken colt or fractious steer shunted aside. But colt, cow or hard-faced stranger were all the same to a barrel-chested Joker. When its master said jump, it jumped like a jackrabbit.

The tremendous impact of the horse leaping forward and striking the gunman squarely with its chest saw the man's muddied boots leave the ground and he was flung backwards with a bellow of fright and rage to crash onto his back, his momentum causing him to somersault completely and finish up on hands and knees in a daze. Unhurriedly, Duane moved the horse forward and swung low to scoop up the fallen rifle.

'Get up and lead the way on down to headquarters,' he ordered. 'Whatever story you've got you can tell Mr Everson. Come on, up, damn you! I don't have all day.'

Somehow the man struggled to his feet. Blood streamed from nose and mouth and he looked somehow broken. Babbling, he tried to explain, to ask questions. He was wasting his time. Known as a quiet man both here and down south, Duane didn't want to talk; instead he poked the fellow sharply in the back of the neck with his own rifle to get him travelling downslope.

So it was that, following eight years of voluntary exile, the second son of the wealthiest man in Bear Lake County returned without warning to Cloud Valley astride a hard-eyed black horse prodding a battered and bleeding man ahead of him with a naked rifle. It wasn't how he'd expected to return, nor the way anyone who knew him might imagine he ever would.

There was no need to announce himself. Long before he reached the sprawling headquarters yard, the whole place was wide awake and even the dogs were barking that 'Rider' Duane was back.

He'd never been comfortable in the room they called the den, had always considered it too big, too grand and much too reflective of his father's personality to be anything but ostentatious and overdone, and today it was somehow darker and gloomier than he remembered despite all the hothouse flowers on display.

Most people were fascinated by this inner sanctum, particularly that brand of wannabee guest whom Jordan liked to entertain here: the young huckster on the way up, the social climber with aspirations, the budding politician eager to ingratiate himself with the strong man of the county. And, of course, the women. Whether married, separated, single or whatever his status might be at any given time, Jordan Everson had always been involved with women. These were often young and were invariably dazzled by his attentions and the overt display of wealth such as many of them had never encountered before.

Typically, Jordan was taking his own sweet time making an appearance. But he was not about to take offence. The unsmiling housekeeper – a stranger to him as were so many at the headquarters now – had at least been able to inform him that, yes, Mr Jordan was still alive, but no, he had not been in the best of health recently.

He'd felt a great weight lift from his shoulders to hear this. For his fear had been that his father's failure to attend several vital high-echelon meetings both in business and political circles in recent times might indicate something seriously amiss at Cloud Valley, hence his decision to break his vow never to return, and saddle up.

The timber titan, rancher and political kingmaker had never been close to his second son by his first wife, which was why there'd been no contact between them over the past eight years.

Duane knew exactly why he was here. But he

hadn't told anyone and likely never would.

The French clock on the overmantel chimed the hour. From the distance could be heard the shouting of the hands working at the corrals. Trailing smoke, Duane made his way over an expanse of Brussels carpet to reach the east window and looked out. Even the outbuildings of Cloud Valley were larger and far better constructed than most people's homes. Nothing new about this. But what was new was the acre upon acre of horseyards and corrals enclosed by gleaming white fences, and the horses wherever he looked.

He expected he'd find out what had switched his father's focus to horses in due course. If he was here long enough, that was. No guarantee that that would be the case. They'd parted on the worst of terms, and to rub salt into Jordan's wounds, his elder brother and apple of his father's eye, Jesse, had up and quit Cloud Valley just a few months following his own departure, leaving the big man with just Tyran and Beth, his children by his second wife, who was also long gone from Cloud Valley.

He'd seen no sign of his half-brother and sister since his arrival an hour earlier. Maybe they'd also left home, he mused, as he turned away from the window. Whoever attested that their father was not a difficult man to get along with had never met him.

Trail-muddied boots marking the soft carpet, he circled the shadowed room with mounting impatience. What in tarnation was Jordan trying to prove, keeping him hanging about like this anyway? He was growing peeved but was determined not to let it show. He'd always been the quiet one of the clan, in contrast to his siblings, particularly Jesse. Jesse was a dynamic replica of their father. Both were capital W Winners and limelighters who just naturally assumed command of any stage they happened to occupy; there was not one jot of reserve or uncertainty in either man's makeup.

'So, it's true. You are back.'

He turned sharply.

His father had appeared soundlessly from the hall-way door to stand before him with one hand in the slash pocket of tailored twill pants, a cigar jutting from his mouth. For a moment a relieved Duane thought the commanding figure appeared just as vigorous as he'd done back in the seventies. But this was only an illusion attributable to poor lighting. Jordan might appear just as tall, haughty and immac-ulately attired as ever, but Duane quickly saw the handsome face was ravaged and that he was leaning on a silver-topped cane as as he came slowly forward. This was a sick man, and Duane felt something almost akin to sympathy as the distance closed between them. Then he read his father's expression and that sentiment fled.

'How do you do?' Jordan's voice had lost none of its resonance, nor the perfunctory handshake any of its power. 'Please be seated.'

He was being treated like a stranger, with formal politeness.

'I'll stand,' he said expressionlessly. It was a bad start and was destined to go downhill from there. Plainly, nothing had changed in eight years. He realized he was a fool for imagining it could have been different.

In answer to his father's brusque query, Duane said,

'I keep tabs on you in the press. When I realized you'd missed some important meetings I got worried.' He spread his hands. 'That's why I came.'

'You could have written.'

'Would you have answered?'

'Most likely not.'

Silence again. The tension was almost tangible. They'd moved from the den to the wide east gallery furnished with massive, rough-hewn pine tables and chairs, adorned with more wildflowers and dimmed by yellow canvas blinds drawn against the bright sun. Here there were framed daguerreotypes of family members, and even a shot of Duane sitting a horse, naturally. There was another on a bureau in the far corner which kept drawing his eye as he sat perched on a bar stool.

Nothing more was said until Duane cleared his throat.

'You look bad.'

'I feel great.'

That was his father. No weaknesses. Always on top.

'You've lost weight,' Duane continued stubbornly.

'They say you can't fatten a thoroughbred.'

This was proving even tougher than he'd expected. He changed his tack.

'Speaking of thoroughbreds, I've been admiring your stock. The Valley is a horse ranch now. How come?'

The formidable eyes focused directly upon him at last. Jordan's expression showed he was losing patience with the verbal fencing.

'All right, I'll admit I've been a little off-colour of late. So?'

It was a grudging and prickly concession but

Duane was quick to go with it.

'I knew it. What's ailing you?' he wanted to know.

'It's a mystery. I began experiencing abdominal pains several months ago and nobody seems able to identify what it is, much less treat it.'

'Not even Doc Greenlease? He's the best man in the county.'

'That fraud!' The older man rubbed his midsection with a scowl. Then he said, 'Why'd you do Turk that way?'

'What?'

'The fellow you attacked up on the switchback. I don't see you for years, and then you announce your arrival by mistreating one of my hands.'

'He's a hand?' At last he was stung. 'He acted more like a gun dog and I treated him as such. What the tarnal was he doing skulking up there in the dark like that anyway? What's going on here?' Duane pointed as a man sporting a double gunrig and puffing a cigar strolled by beyond the gardens, as he'd seen him do several times already. 'And what's that joker supposed to be about anyway? I've seen banks in California with half the security you've got here.'

'We've had troubles, that's all you need know.' Jordan shifted uncomfortably on the sofa and scowled. 'You claim you knew I was ill from the newspapers. How could that be so? There's been nothing in the newspapers, I saw to that.'

'I know. I have the Bear Lake County News delivered so as to keep tabs.'

A flicker of surprise disturbed his father's formidable features. It was quickly erased.

'Why?'

Duane ignored that. 'When I read where you'd

missed a number of the important meetings you usually chair, I wired Sheriff Tune in town and he told me you'd been almost housebound for weeks. See? No mystery.'

The housekeeper reappeared at that point, toting a tray. A handsome unsmiling woman in her middle forties with glossy dark hair drawn severely back into a tight bun, she placed a tray upon a low table between the two men. The woman didn't speak, but it seemed to Duane she hesitated several moments too long, her dark gaze flickering from one to the other as though in disapproval. She retired with a rustle of starched petticoats beneath a no-nonsense quakercloth dress.

Maybe it's me, Duane mused sardonically as he picked up a coffee. Apart from one or two old hands, he didn't seem to be impressing anyone, not even the hired help.

He placed a coffee before his father, who ignored it. Instead Jordan produced and lighted a fresh stogie. He coughed, grimaced and clawed at his midsection.

'Fit as stud bull,' he attested to divert comment. Then, 'Your brother ever visit you in Arizona?'

He knew he meant Jesse.

'No.' He sipped his coffee. 'How come he quit Cloud Valley as well?'

'Got too big to live in my shadow is my guess.' The ghost of a smile touched the haggard face. 'Too much like his old man for his own good, that one.' The smile faded. 'Is that what made you leave too? Felt you couldn't compete?'

'Just got to that footloose age, I guess,' he drawled casually. 'Do you hear anything of Jesse these days?'

'Doing fairly well for himself down in Wyoming last I heard.'

'I was surprised to hear he'd left too.'

Jordan's expression changed dramatically as he got to his feet. 'I think it's called the rats deserting the sinking ship disease.'

'You were sinking? You, the owner of the biggest lumber and mining operations in the county with enough money to buy whatever you wanted: land, votes, horses.' Duane hesitated, then couldn't help himself. 'And more women than you could poke a stick at.'

'Damn your impertinence, mister!' Jordan made to propel himself towards him, but pain wracked his face and he slumped against the piano, the immaculately garbed wreckage of a powerful man. 'You never forgave me for remarrying after your mother died, did you?' he rasped accusingly. 'Never!'

Duane swung away to hide his hurt. His mother was one of several reasons behind his return. She had been married to this man, had loved him. He owed it to her to come back, not to Jordan Gene Everson.

Deliberately now he moved to the bureau and picked up the framed picture. The grainy photograph portrayed a family group standing in bright sunlight before a modest cabin backdropped by piney woods. The man with one arm carelessly draped round the shoulders of the darkly attractive young woman was Jordan Everson in his youth, rugged, confident, protecting. Before the couple stood two young boys, one a fair-headed replica of the father and the smaller child strongly favouring the mother.

He'd thought of this picture often over his years in

exile, sometimes wishing he'd taken it with him. Even now, some twenty years on since they'd lived and struggled over at the old place in the canyon, and despite all the turbulence that had marred their lives, it still seemed to him that the happiness reflected in this shot taken by a travelling photographer was genuine. His gaze lingered on Simone as he replaced the picture. He turned his head to find his father staring at him challengingly.

He's waiting for me to say something he can take offence at, he mused. Something about Ma, most likely.

'That fellow I tangled with,' he remarked softly. 'Turk. He told me the twins' mother left you too.'

Jordan lifted a hand, let it drop.

'She wanted to go, I didn't try to stop her. She's remarried and living in the Dakotas, so I hear.'

'Guess I'm surprised there isn't a third Mrs Everson by this.'

Jordan flinched. They traded glares. The chasm separating them yawned even wider. Both were angry, but Jordan didn't swallow his emotions as his son often tended to do.

'It won't make a blind bit of difference, you know?' he said deliberately.

Duane frowned in puzzlement. 'Huh? What are you talking about?'

'The will, mister! You'd better understand your coming back won't see me change one thing. It's all cut, dried and finalized if I croak.'

Duane felt a hot flush sting his cheekbones.

'You think that's why I'm here?'

'I'm a realist, boy, always have been. I'm rich and might die. I wouldn't blame you for showing up to make sure you hadn't been overlooked in the final draft.'

That hurt. He glanced at his father in the quiet and seemed to detect a hint of shame in his face at what he'd said, or maybe this was just his imagination.

Finally, Jordan was forced to speak again. His tone was almost conciliatory.

'I appreciate your coming all the way from the south. But I'll be fine, so there's nothing holding you.'

'I'll be staying on a spell.'

'What?'

'Hey, yeah, what's that you're saying, brother?' a voice broke in.

Duane swung as the youthful couple ducked in beneath the yellow awnings and came towards him, smiling and extending their arms in greeting. Tyran and Beth had been children when he went away, now the twins were nineteen, both slender and comely and favouring their mother. It was a fact of life that he'd never felt close to his half-brother and sister either, although their welcome to him now seemed genuine enough.

'We've been eavesdropping from the stoop,' good-looking Tyran confessed with a cheeky half-grin at his father. Then he winked at Duane. 'So, what brings you back, Rider? I mean, really?'

'Your dad can explain.' Suddenly Duane was weary, bone-aching, played-out and beat. Too many miles and way too much tension for one day. He arched an eyebrow at his father. 'And I'm still staying on. Where do I put up?'

'We don't have much spare room at the moment,'

replied the master of a twenty-room mansion.

'Perhaps Duane would feel more at home in the bunkhouse,' smiled Beth, pursing her lips with a mock frown as she raked his travel-grimed figure from head to heels with eyes of clearest baby blue. 'Just jesting, of course, big brother.'

'That's not funny, Sis,' Tyran chided. But Duane prevented anyone saying more.

'I'll bunk in the stables,' he declared, making for the doors. 'Won't be the first time.' He fitted his battered trail-hat to his head and his features were totally expressionless as he touched fingers to the brim. 'Really great to be back.'

The trio watched him go in silence then moved as one to the huge shadowed windows to follow his slender horseman's figure crossing the immaculately kept yards and lawns. Their eyes seemed full of secrets and unasked questions as they turned to stare at one another. Caution held them quiet for a moment; suspicion sped their thoughts.

2

Welcome

Turk's face looked like raw meat.

'This just ain't fair, Mr Everson.'

'Don't talk to me about fair, mister. I've got a pain in my guts that just won't go away. You should gripe. How much did I say you have coming?'

'Forty dollars and thirty-five cents, sir,' supplied the ranch bookkeeper, thrusting a small pile of notes and coins across the desk towards the battered hardcase. Then he took up a pen, dipped the nib in the inkpot and drew a neat red line through a name in his ledger and scrawled: Services terminated. He glanced up from behind wire-framed pince nez. 'Anything else, ex-bodyguard?'

Breathing hard, Turk scooped up the money. The man was bristling with offence and there was blood in his eye as he cut a sideways glance at the tall figure standing by the office window, gazing out. His brute pride was affronted by his summary dismissal.

'You could give a man another chance, Mr Everson. I never let you down afore yesterday.'

Everson drained his whiskey glass with a grimace. The day was not an hour old, yet this was his second. Sometimes whiskey was the only thing that helped.

'Once is once too often,' he stated flatly. 'My son could have been a murderer on his way in to slit my throat.'

'But this ain't fair, boss.'

Irritated at last, Jordan Everson talked straight.

'Mister, you were hired on reputation. You're supposed to be capable. That's why we assigned you to the ridges. It's rough country up there, just the sort of route some backshooter hunting me might elect to take, as happened last month. All right, so someone does turn up through the tall and uncut. But this is no assassin, just my son come home to visit with me in case I croak. Yet he jumped you, mashed you up and hauled you down here like a whipped dog.' He spread his hands. 'He's just a horseman, for God's sake. What chance would you have had against some two-gun heller with a knife between his teeth?'

'Mr Everson, I reckon that Duane is one hell of a lot more than he looks. And who'd have expected a damned hoss to jump on a man thataway? Like a trained hound dog, so he was.'

Turk broke off as a figure appeared in the doorway. The pie-faced, dark-garbed heavyweight with the walnut handle of Colt .45 jutting up from his waistband was, like himself, a member of Cloud Valley's newly acquired security force. He had eyes like chipped rock and a mean reputation.

'You were saying?' Jordan murmured without taking his eyes from the scene outside.

Turk was smarter than he looked. He knew when his hand was all played out. Face burning, he jammed on his hat and stepped past the man in the doorway to disappear with a heavy clump of bootheels.

The second man left and Jordan poured himself another.

'What the devil is going on out there?' he demanded as the sounds from the corrals grew louder. 'We don't have any breaking work scheduled for today, do we?'

'No, sir.'

Jordan narrowed his eyes and leaned closer to the glass. 'Then what are all those men doing down there. . . ? Never mind, I'll see for myself.'

'Are you sure you should be stepping outdoors so early, sir?'

The clerk was talking to himself. Energized by irritation, Everson was already walking down the corridor to quit the house and head downslope for the corrals, which he reached just in time to witness something special.

Perched high on the back of a quarter horse stallion as he bucked and plunged his furious way round the breaking corral with a dozen cowboys and yard hands bawling encouragement, Duane glimpsed his father from the corner of his eye but prudently concentrated on the job in hand as Barsheeba Nightsong dropped four hoofs back to ground and started whirling in a tight circle, well over a thousand pounds of concentrated rage.

The stud-horse had proven one of Cloud Valley's prime assets as a sire, but had been earning his keep on the spread for two full years without ever having been broken to saddle and bridle. Early on, the stallion's unrideable reputation had proven a magnet and a challenge attracting breakers from all over the county, but not any more. Even the champion reinsmen had long given up on Barsheeba Nightsong and it was six months since any reckless rider had even attempted to throw a leg across his bad-tempered back.

Now an excited waddy with a stopwatch was bawling, 'Thirty seconds, by God!' And Jordan Everson was watching so intently he forgot the constant pain behind his silver belt-buckle for just a brief while.

It was a ride to watch and remember. The stud reared so violently that at times he appeared in danger of toppling backwards. When he switched tactics to sunfish round the enclosure he did so with breedy neck bowed, the ears laid back and big teeth bared. He was doing his damnedest to sink his teeth into the rider's right leg. But seemingly effortlessly, Duane continued to keep his leg barely out of reach while using heels and knees to goad the animal into greater efforts.

Barsheeba was swift and strong and mean as snake juice. The animal had had plenty of opportunity to hone his cowboy-crippling talents over the years, to put a polish on his full bunch of tricks. Quick as lightning now, he whipped his head around to snap at Duane's other leg. He came so close this time he left tooth marks in the boot which set all the watchers yelling afresh.

Furious that one of his best gambits had failed, the lathered bay tucked his tail and bogged his head to go storming round the perimeter of the corral yet again, pitching and bawling in the most wicked display of equine bad temper Cloud Valley had ever witnessed.

But the rider was a burr, a rocking armchair loafer

as nonchalantly unshakeable as though he were attached to the saddle with big anchor straps. The horse threw everything he had left into that final sequence. He pitched forward, sideways then spun in viciously tight circles. He crawfished, backed up, became airborne. And each time he came down he did so with his legs as stiff as pistons, hitting the earth so hard that the impact could be felt as far away as the house where figures now lined the east gallery, watching and marvelling at both horse and horsemanship.

Until abruptly it was all over, the stud standing with all four legs splayed wide, head hanging low and breath rasping like a broken bellows. He didn't even make a token nip as the horseman slid from the saddle, seemed deaf to the spontaneous cheers of the onlookers.

Most of those present had never clapped eyes on Duane Everson until that morning; now they knew exactly who he was and what he could do, had no trouble understanding why some of the veteran hands called him Rider.

Clambering atop the fence, Duane glanced round but his father was gone. This didn't bother him. The fact that Jordan had made the effort to come down to the yards at all was something he found encouraging, suggesting his condition might not be quite as bad as he'd feared. As he jumped to ground, the ramrod passed him a swab of cotton waste to mop off the sweat, and the head wrangler joined the pair as they headed up the slope for the bunkhouse where the temperamental cook was now clanging the triangle furiously to remind them breakfast was running late.

'You know, I had a hunch if anyone could bust that mean mustang it had to be you, Duane.'

The grizzled head wrangler was grinning ear to ear. It had been at his suggestion that the new occupant of the stables' comfortable bunk-room had agreed to 'take a crack' at Barsheeba Nightsong on his first full day back on the Valley.

'I reckon I enjoyed that about as much as he did,' Duane replied, glancing back. He was sweating, dust-coated and feeling good. Yesterday had been tense and exhausting but today seemed to be kicking off just right. But he wasn't seeking acclaim, didn't expect it. He'd lived seventeen years in his brother's shadow here, and both of them were always over-shadowed by their father. He wasn't courting popularity here, just acceptance.

He switched his glance to the house to see the slender figures of the twins standing together on the patio. Seemed that they preferred one another's company in young adulthood just as they'd done as toddle-aged kids playing around his and Jesse's legs. He felt a vague twinge of guilt that somehow he'd never been close to Tyran and Beth, mainly, he supposed, because he'd resented their mother taking the place of Ma when Jordan remarried.

'Mebbe now that heller's had his tail feathers singed he won't be so inclined to give the boys trouble every time they try and work with him,' remarked the ramrod. 'And that's saying something, considering the fact he was the first stud your dad imported when we switched from cattle to horses, so that's going back six or seven years that the boys have been getting kicked, bit and bucked off by that varmint.'

'Had him that long, huh?' Duane replied. 'So tell

me, what prompted Jordan to make the big changeover to horses, Lee?'

'No idea, Rider. You know your dad even better than me. When he decides to do a thing he just goes ahead and does it; he don't hold any committee meeting.'

He nodded absently as he sucked in a couple of calming breaths and surveyed one of the finest sights a man could ever see. Jordan had built his palatial headquarters on a plateau between two gentle hills at the head of a valley just a hundred yards below the timberline. The house commanded a panoramic view of rolling grazelands which began well up in the foothills then extended far out onto the Great Plains where they were eventually bordered some two miles distant by Buffalo Creek on its journey out of the mountains to link up with the Red Warrior.

Majestic forests climbed the sky beneath the early sun that shimmered off the lake where Jordan had often taken his more important guests out boating and fishing.

As always, the spread both impressed and sobered him, now perhaps even more so than when he'd left. Yet there was still that mysterious something about the very beauty and opulence of Cloud Valley that could sometimes touch the skin like a cold hand. His skin, that was. He would be first to admit that he'd never stopped unfavourably comparing the grandeur of this place with the more spartan life the clan had known on Suspicion Canyon's rough grass.

Breakfast at the bunkhouse was pleasant enough. Plainly the men were a little restrained to find themselves sharing their sourdough flapjacks and powerful camp-fire coffee with an Everson. There was curiosity in the glances directed his way, but he doubted they had half as many questions they'd like answered as did he. He'd returned home to find his father possibly seriously ill, his half-brother and sister swanning round in elegant town clothes like privileged visitors, and a whole raft of new faces on the payroll backed up by a squad of some six or seven heavily armed men whose job it plainly was to guard the headquarters, against just what he wasn't quite sure.

He knew he could ask questions. He'd never been one of the boys here, that role having been created and exploited to the hilt by Jesse. Yet there were one or two left he could trust, like the ramrod and straw boss whose welcome back had been as warm and satisfying as his family's had been reserved. Most likely they could tell him whatever he might want to know.

He might do that. Later. Not now. He was a self-sufficient man who relied more on what he saw, felt, figured out or could prove rather than on hearsay or gossip. Mostly, that was. There was the odd person he trusted enough to rely on anything they might tell him. Like Chinook.

Quitting the cookhouse an hour later, his eyes were on the western rim where the soaring timbered tiers of Drumgriff Basin chopped the sky, mighty forest monarchs rippling in the spring wind. The basin was where the money was made. He planned on taking a ride up there and likely other places as well, both to get the feel of the home acres again and to give Cloud Valley a little time and space to adjust to the notion of his being back.

Even without their saying so he knew people were

trying to guess how long he intended staying on, even why he was back, particularly in view of the fact that he'd made a vow never to return following his last blazing row with his father all those years ago.

A humourless smile worked his mouth as he entered the cool gloom of the stables. The truth was, he couldn't honestly answer anybody's questions on those subjects for the simple reason even he didn't know how long he would be staying on. He only knew why.

He led Joker out of the stall and set about grooming his tough black hide in the sunlight. As he worked he caught a quick flash of light coming off something in the timber above the lake, thought it could be caused by sunlight glinting off metal or glass; maybe something like field-glasses. And then when he glanced across carefully trimmed lawns and gardens, a curtain in the mansion's west wing twitched and fell still. He didn't know whether to scowl or smile.

Sitting his mount on a hillside on the south rim of Drumgriff Basin forty-eight hours later, Duane had the feeling that, apart from the vast grey areas of naked stumps where forests had once stood, the profit-making arm of the Everson empire appeared pretty much as it had been when he'd seen it last.

There was the same air of bustling activity up along the far slopes where husky buckers and fallers were shrunk to midget figures by distance as they went about the business of slaughtering the mighty oaks, pines and sequoias for trimming and snagging out by ox teams down to the vast holding ponds along Missoula Creek. From there they were floated southward a mile before being set loose to make their headlong way over the man-made spillway which carried them swiftly all the tumbling, cascading way down to the junction with the Red Warrior River, from which point they made their more leisurely meandering way south-east to the company sawmills at Arrowhead.

The smell of sawdust and stink of smoke rising from the donkey engines blended with the pure mountain air, and it was the scent of progress. Progress. Just another word, idea or notion upon which he and Jordan had never seen eye to eye. But why should he expect it to be otherwise? They'd managed to disagree on almost everything that mattered in their lives, so why not the main family business?

He smoked a cigarette through as, with one leg hooked over his pommel, he sat lazily studying the toiling men, animals and machines far below. He appeared to be dreaming a little in the balmy sunshine but was actually noting everything he saw, like an accountant totting up figures. By the time he was through he knew the work force at the basin was roughly double the strength it had been when he'd left, as one would expect, whereas security up here, in marked contrast to Cloud Valley, appeared to have shrunk.

He nodded as though in confirmation of a suspicion, spoke to the borrowed bay, then set off along a lateral trail for Sawtooth Point. He'd needed to know if the ranch's beefed-up security was general throughout his father's holdings or otherwise. The obvious fact that it was not suggested that the presence of gunpackers down on the home acres was prompted less by concerns for property than for persons, or a person. One person was his guess. His father. So how come it seemed the most powerful and influential figure in Bear Lake County appeared to be living in fear for his safety?

Maybe Chinook, the old mountain man, could shed some light as to why this should be so.

The timber cruisers' road he followed with such easy familiarity sliced at a tangent down and across the wooded foothills which lifted in thousand-foot terraces to meet the granite majesty of Heaven's Rim, which in turn was topped out by the green of Casper's Plateau with the snow-white fangs of the Divide floating dreamily in the distance.

Despite his reputation as a serious and sober man, Duane felt a sense of almost childlike excitement as the landmark feature of Sawtooth Point abruptly thrust its stone finger into the sky ahead. He'd ridden up here first as a kid with his father and Jesse, and Jordan had often left him with the oldster while he went off hunting for bearwolf or deer with his Big Fifty rifle.

The boys had promptly tabbed Chinook 'a man to ride the river with', an expression precocious Jesse had just come by.

The mountain man had been old, white, grizzled and tough as wang and rawhide the day they first met him. He still looked exactly the same when Duane rode into his camp and jumped down, both of them laughing like fools as they hooted, hugged and howled, mountain man style.

It was good to reminisce, and they gave it full rein. But by the time they were finishing off Chinook's palate-exalting venison stew the old man had clearly scented out the concerns that had brought him up here.

'Might as well quit blowin' on the fur and git to the hide, Rider,' he grunted, pausing to service his teeth with a six-inch pick.

It was Chinook who'd handed him his nickname the first day he saw him as a curly-headed button sitting the saddle of a half-wild eighteen hands mustang stallion as calmly as if it were a child's pony. He squinted, bringing into play a vast network of weather wrinkles fanning away from eyes as clear as a basin brook.

'So just what is it you want to know?' he pressed. 'Or can I guess? Would it be concernin' your daddy, mebbe? About who's tryin' to rub him out, and why?'

Meeting that clear-eyed stare, Duane nodded.

'Knew you'd understand.' He set his bowl aside, leaned back and took out the makings. 'All right, old-timer. Go ahead and tell me all you know, suspect or just plain guess about Jordan and anyone and anything else that might be connected. I'll sift through it all later.'

The sun was westering over the Divide as Duane quit to follow the tumbling, brawling trace of Buffalo Creek on its steep downslope journey from the basin to Suspicion Canyon an hour later. He rode easy in the saddle but his expression lightened and darkened as he travelled, the shape and shadow of his intent reflections revealed in his face.

The old mountain man had been blunt. Whilst readily acknowledging the fact that he never visited Cloud Valley, Chinook still felt he understood enough of what was going on there to put forward a reasonably informed opinion.

It was his considered belief that someone was out 'to get' Duane's father, as he put it. He was deeply disturbed by Jordan's mystery illness plus the fact that he'd dismissed Doc Greenlease, as well as the 'odd mix' of people surrounding him these days. Then there was the reality that Jordan had been shot at by persons unknown recently, which was the first Duane had heard about this. As well there was a number of strange and unexplained incidents associated with the spread over recent months which had resulted in an increasingly isolated and suspicious Jordan adding a bunch of gunpacking bodyguards and nighthawks to his payroll. For Chinook, all this tallied as proof positive that something sinister was going on, and he reckoned Duane's showing up out of the past was about as timely as anything could be.

The bay missed its footing on watercressed rock as they recrossed the joyous, burbling creek beneath the shadow of a mighty oak which had been old when Lewis and Clark drove westward across pristine Montana away to the south back in 1805. He righted the horse without effort but from there on concentrated more on the trail and less upon the scenery.

This was prettier country than anything he'd seen in Arizona or in between. With the momentum of its fall from the basin, the Buffalo cascaded swiftly into eddying pools, rushed through the rapids or went weaving silkily through quieter passages where ancient gnarled boughs intertwined overhead and reached low, forcing the rider to duck his head and Joker to roll his eyes whitely at the gloom.

Then out into the fast-fading sunlight again to traverse a widening gorge lined with stately cedars. Here the lichen grew thick and green on smooth boulders, or hung down from branches like old elves' green whiskers, reminding him vividly of the Old Country tales Ma had told them 'way back when.

Within a half-mile the stream broadened into a creek again and he was travelling Suspicion Canyon once again in the deepening dusk.

His face was blank as he raised the ruins of the old house on the cottonwood hill, used his knees to swing his mount in that direction. Memories crowded in but he was easy with them now. Different from the way he'd been for years following Simone Duchamp Everson's death from cholera at the age of just twenty-nine years .

One thing he was proud of in respect of that bitter period was that he'd never blamed Jordan in any way over his mother's loss. It was a comforting claim to be able to make, considering the gap that had always existed between father and son in just about every other aspect of their uneasy lives together.

He swung down by what remained of the house gate. Here the past beat like a shadowy tide. What remained of the house stood on the breast of a smooth grassy hill. Built largely of rough-hewn lumber and adobe mud by his father's own hands, when he was too poor to afford anything better, the dun-coloured walls had long since caved in unevenly and grass and weed grew high around them.

Night was drawing on. The warmth of the day faded fast and an uneasy wind came snaking across meadows and pastures where his father, tall, robust and powerful, had husbanded his scrubber cattle herd with such zealousness before he began forming timber combines and buying up timber leases, from which point his progress had been spectacular.

In his mind's eye he saw Jordan striding about the old place with Jesse at his heels; Jordan and Jesse laughing together as the father happily attempted to teach his elder son to ride a horse the way his younger brother had been able to do almost before he could crawl.

Always together.

Jesse and Jordan. Duane and Simone.

Simone Duchamp's short life had been an epic adventure in a dramatic way such as only a western odyssey could be. Born of French immigrant parents who'd ventured from Mexico to link up with the Oregon Trail many years ago when few dared, she'd seen her mother and father slaughtered by the Cheyenne at Medicine Bow, was subsequently taken in by the tribe and spent the next ten years of her life living as an Indian child before being rescued by the soldiers at the battle of Coyote Crossing on the Wyoming border.

Adopted and raised by the Mormons, Simone had almost lived down her 'Injun' past by the time she met and married Jordan Everson and, as far as her second son was aware, had lived a fulfilling if spartan life right here where he was standing until the day she died.

She was buried over by the oak which still trailed from one of its lower limbs time-yellowed fragments of the rope on which a boisterous Jesse Everson and his kid brother had swung seemingly eternally, in the bluebonnet summers of another age, another life.

He replaced his hat and looped the bay's reins over his arm to approach the grave. Bedding birds were squalling in the darkening trees and the last of the daylight was draining away in the west as he tramped past what remained of the hip-roofed barn.

There was no warning.

One moment he was stepping over a rotting dead-fall, the next the horse was going up on its hind legs with a scream and splashing great gouts of blood over him as the deep-throated roar of a rifle split the night's hush.

He went to ground so fast he was burrowing behind the deadfall and raking Colt from leather while the horse's body was still rolling downslope, its slack limbs and lolling head telling him it had died on its feet.

He'd been shot at once before during a rustling raid on his horse-ranch in California. It was some-thing a man never got used to. Duane was cursing, sweating and kicking his way behind a gnarled elbow of the deadfall when the repeater rifle spoke three times in rapid succession, gunflashes flaring wickedly from the gulch a hundred yards off to his left.

Training gunsights on the flashes, he triggered once then shifted position again. The rifle responded and the oak elbow exploded under the impact of smashing lead.

This bastard could really shoot!

Desperately conscious of his precarious position, Duane rolled left, touched off a snap shot then violently spun away in the opposite direction, hugging mother earth passionately as retaliatory lead now raked the grass where he'd lain moments before. The gloom was deepening fast, but he knew he couldn't rely upon darkness for protection. He must get to the horse and the Winchester in the saddle scabbard.

He turned his head. It looked a mile to the bulked

mass of the body, but he knew it could be no more than thirty feet. The potential irony in his being shot to death within yards of his mother's resting place didn't enter his head as he sprang erect. His mind was blank. He was now acting on pure intuition, and with the self-survival instinct fuelling his boilers as never before went streaking away in a low zigzagging run with lead hornets zipping around his tucked-in head and flying boot-heels.

The dead horse loomed close.

He covered the remaining distance in a headlong dive, his left hand snaking out to snatch at the stock of the rifle. The weapon hissed from leather as his momentum carried him on over the horse's flanks to execute an automatic tumble-turn that threw him flat in the coarse grass beyond.

Bullets slammed harmlessly into the animal's body as Duane jacked a shell into the chamber. His breath tore in his lungs yet he was calmer now, lethally so. Hunting was his passion and he was in full hunting mode as he willed his body to steadiness, achieved it, then snaked belly-flat through the grass to snatch a quick look round the bay's bloodied muzzle.

He could see nothing, yet the sound of a steel-shod hoof clipping stone carried clearly.

The drygulcher was hightailing.

His reaction was immediate. He knew that gulch of his childhood as well as he knew his own name. Springing to his feet, he streaked across to the tree, automatically calculating how long it would take his quarry to reappear. He figured the gulch to be some seventy yards long; the horse was now running at a fast lope. Putting the Winchester to his shoulder, he cuddled the silky oak stock against his cheek and squinted along the barrel at the barely visible far end of the gulch, counting deliberately to seven, then he started in shooting.

With the rifle bucking against his shoulder and gunsmoke billowing wildly in the wind, he feared for a moment he'd guessed wrong as the night-dimmed lip of the gulch remained empty. But he kept on levering and triggering until suddenly there was the blurred yet definable bulk of horse and crouched rider exploding onto open rangeland to go rocketing away at a headlong gallop.

Duane was no longer shooting for effect. He notched the foresight with his hindsight then trailed the fast-receding figure for one long steadying breath, and gently squeezed trigger.

The ragged cry of a man hard hit sent a tingle down his spine. Swiftly he worked another round into the chamber but didn't get to fire. There was no longer anything to see, nothing to hear but the rhythmic thrum of receding hoofbeats.

Slowly he lowered the weapon to ground and leaned his weight upon it. He could still hear the gun echoes fading away into mountain silences. No birds called and he was alone in the final dregs of the daylight. Only the long grass moved in the wind.

3

Mystery Range

It was almost midnight before he raised the lights of headquarters at the end of a six-mile trek afoot across Little Round Top followed by the final two miles doubling up with a nighthawk from the north graze astride his paint pony.

Not that he was complaining. The sniper at Suspicion Canyon had done his damnedest to kill him and he knew he was lucky to be alive.

Nonetheless he was still feeling pretty played out and edgy on reaching the home acres, and certainly wasn't expecting what met the eye as they rode wearily in beneath the title gate. The whole mansion was ablaze with lights, with the beat of a throbbing guitar accompanied by banjo and piano flooding out from open windows and doors to engulf them as the weary hand hauled his horse to a halt by the front gallery. The horse arched its neck in a sudden toss, reflecting the lights in the moist jewels of its eyes as Duane climbed stiffly down.

'What's going on?' he puzzled. 'Some kind of party?'

'Guess you could call it that,' the man said enigmatically. He swung the horse's head and was gone, heading back for the pasture for a further six-hour vigil of cold, boredom and the company of dumb critters which at least were smart enough to spend their nights sleeping. A vampire kept better hours than a nightrider on Cloud Valley these troubled days.

Duane weaved a little as he made his way along the paved pathway. His feet were giving him hell; a horseman loathes walking and he'd walked plenty. A figure appeared from behind the marble fountain with its heroic Grecian figures bowed beneath cascading waters. The lanky sentry with his hand on his gunbutt had to look twice at this limping, trail-grimed figure before recognition hit. He stepped aside wordlessly, leaving Duane to continue on with the lights throwing his shadow hugely behind him.

Approaching the steps he noted the stylish coach parked over by the barn. The bleary driver paced stolidly to and fro nearby, swinging his arms to maintain circulation in the chilly midnight hour.

He removed his hat as he crossed the gallery and went directly through into the front room. He halted abruptly. Before him, beneath the shimmering lights of the chandelier, with music provided by a cowboy band of five assembled on the upper landing, his father, impressive in elegant evening wear with medals on his lapel, was close-dancing stylishly with a gorgeous blonde in a low-cut gown of shimmering off-white organza. With sequins.

The cowboys stopped playing as abruptly as if

someone had thrown a switch. Duane didn't realize just what an apparition he presented. A shirtsleeve had ripped and snagged during the gun battle. Wood fragments had peppered the side of his neck. Dried horse's blood streaked his shirt and pants, and his face. Mist-soaked, muddied and squinting in the brilliant light of the chandelier, he looked more like the survivor of a train wreck than the neat and sober Rider.

Gliding flamboyantly over waxed floorboards where the carpets had been rolled back and furniture shifted to the walls to afford the dancers full scope, Jordan and his glamorous partner slid to a flourishing halt by the piano, not realizing the cause of the interruption until they turned and saw him.

The silence held for a long moment as Duane tiredly dragged off his sodden hat and hung it by the throat strap off his sixgun. He felt a sneer flicker along the edge of his mind as he realized that, unexpected though this spectacle might be, he was not really surprised. Why should he be? This was pure Jordan. Far more so than any man he'd ever known, his father had always done exactly what he liked, when he liked and with whomever he chose; and if the rest of the world didn't like it they could go fry. The fact that he was ailing, under pressure, isolated and suspicious of everyone to an almost manic degree, a degree that had seen him dismiss his physician and end up foolishly relying upon just the twins and his housekeeper to nurse him, didn't mean that he'd discarded the eccentric, unpredictable and often affronting habits of a lifetime.

'What the blue devil!' Jordan exclaimed, leading his wide-eyed partner across the floor. 'Just what have you been up to, mister?' Then, unexpectedly, he smiled and gestured at his partner. He was wearing white gloves. 'Forgive my manners, my dear. Clarissa, may I present my second son, Duane. I'm sure I must have mentioned him. Duane, Miss Clarissa Harte of the Butte Hartes. Now, don't keep us in suspense, mister. What was it? Got lost? Met a bear? Went to town and got mixed up with some loose women perhaps?'

Duane just stared. Jordan appeared to be under the influence of something, liquor, dope, maybe whatever medication he was now relying upon the unsmiling Mrs Barker to feed him. His eyes were too bright and his smile appeared pasted on. His son knew instantly he wouldn't get any sense out of him tonight; that was certain sure.

'Someone took a shot at me over on the old place at sundown,' he stated calmly. He nodded his head at bluejawed Kraft, Jordan's personal bodyguard. 'I might have winged him. I'd put men out to look for him and make sure there's nobody else about, if I were you.'

'Just a minute!' Jordan hollered, but Duane was on his way out. This horseman wanted a good clean up, a stiff shot and something to soak his feet in. There was nothing for him here right now.

'We'll talk at breakfast,' he called over his shoulder as he left. He glanced up as he went down the steps. The housekeeper and the twins were on the first floor balcony, staring down. They didn't speak, seemed oblivious to Jordan's angry hollering. Kraft barked orders and one of his men went trotting for the bunkhouse to roust some of the high-priced protection out of their warm beds and into their saddles.

The quirley he rolled and lit as he entered the dimly lighted stables tasted the best of the day. As he limped by the stalls an invisible Joker whickered a sleepy greeting. The hostler had left a lamp burning in the snug bunk-room, where he shucked out of his gear, rubbed himself down, then climbed into a faded pair of old denims and a calico shirt before pouring himself a double jolt of Old Turkey.

Easing back into the battered leather chair by the bunk and feeling the blended bourbon begin to warm his belly, he was calm and relaxed, his thinking now clear as blown glass.

In an odd kind of way, he now realized, he almost welcomed the attempt upon his life. Up until the moment the drygulcher opened up on him, he realized now, he'd been metaphorically standing back and absorbing the strangely altered atmosphere of the spread, sifting through all the varying layers of incident, attitudes and changing atmospherics, trying to make sense of it at his own leisurely pace.

With the old man looking so bad and acting so strangely, he'd been beginning to believe that, despite the fact that he claimed to have been shot at once or twice in recent times, Jordan's suspicions and his confinement to the house surrounded by Kraft and his Colt brethren indicated he was deteriorating mentally to such a degree that he could no longer distinguish fact from fantasy, that he could be fast losing the authority and power that made him what he was.

Not any longer.

Nothing could be more real than what had happened back at the canyon. Someone had tried to kill him. And what he'd drawn from this incident, apart from the aches and pains, was the certainty that, regardless of how the old man looked and acted tonight, whatever Jordan was afraid of here was rock-solid real.

Someone was out there with maybe the whole family in his gunsights, and getting them before they got him was now plainly his prime responsibility.

He refilled his glass before stretching out on the bunk. He sighed luxuriously, drawing a woollen blanket over his aching legs. Spring might be flourishing in Montana but the night cold still bit. His eyelids were growing heavy. He was thinking of Alameda Ranch south of Tucson, of the easy, sun-filled rhythms of the days and nights there surrounded by his horses and his friends. There were no chilly nights on his place this time of year; maybe even the hot Santa Ana winds were already beginning to blow.

He brought his thoughts back to the here and now as he felt himself drifting off, made his plans. He would ride down to Doubletree first thing tomorrow. He needed to talk to some people he knew there. Real, solid, everyday kind of people who might give a man sensible answers to straight questions. That breed seemed thin upon the ground up here on Cloud Valley this springtime.

'You call that a kiss, Duane Everson?'

'It will have to do for now.'

'Are you not pleased to see me again?'

'I surely am.'

'Then why the cold fish kiss?'

'Is that what it was?'

'It was not as you kissed me the night before you left.'

'That was eight years ago, Jana. We were just kids then.'

'You were seventeen, I fourteen. We did not kiss like children.'

He had to smile. He should have realized Jana wouldn't have changed. She'd been different from everyone else at the Placer Street school which both attended 'way back when, Mexican-different, with her striking looks and impulsive ways even then. They'd remained casual friends after he quit school to work on the spread while Jesse went off to college in Wyoming. Indeed there'd been a summer when he and Jesse and Jana Castillo, along with other friends from the ranches and town, had seemed constantly in each other's company, swimming, riding, attending dances at the church hall where Jana had been the youngest girl there but was allowed to attend because she looked and acted older than she was.

Studying her now over the rim of his coffee cup at the diner, he knew he'd have to have ice-water in his veins not to be impressed. His hometown back in the Arizonan borderlands was of Spanish American mix, and he'd had Mexican girlfriends from time to time. One or two, he supposed, might be as attractive as the girl seated opposite him with her back to the street now, but none had her personality or vitality. Jana always appeared to have wisdom and under-standing beyond her years. Independent, assured and unconventional, she had an inborn ease with people and situations that allowed her to be exactly as she wanted and somehow get away with it. She attracted men and flirted with them, yet at the same time remained paradoxically detached, singular, unattainable.

It didn't surprise him to discover she hadn't

married, although he was surprised she'd not returned to Mexico following the death of her father. Instead she'd stayed on in the house and followed the oddly assorted careers of sometime teacher, assistant nurse to Doc Greenlease and as much work as she wanted as a singer and dancer at the saloons along Pioneer Street.

He hadn't realized before they'd met up that he needed a friendly face and someone he could trust; today he felt he'd found both.

They'd been cheerfully reminiscing, but now Duane turned serious.

'I came back when I learned Jordan was ill, Jana. He's worse than I expected and the spread's changed so much I hardly recognize it. Not in looks but in the way folks are out there.' He went on to discuss his father's condition, the brooding atmosphere at the mansion, the oddly perplexing closeness of the housekeeper and his half-brother and sister. It was not until he afforded a cryptic account of last night's gunplay at Suspicion Canyon that she reached across the table and squeezed his hand.

'Rider.' His nickname went back to their childhood. 'I have heard much of the strange happenings out there, more than you realize.'

'How so?'

'You do not know I help out Doctor Greenlease when he is busy, as he so often is these days? He says he is *mucho* concerned about your father's health. He was very hurt and very sad when he was dismissed.'

She was right. He hadn't known she worked for the medico, and he knew immediately he must take advantage of that fact. So they quit the eatery together to make their way round to Placer Street where grumpy old Doc received them if not effusively, then at least with some evident improvement on his trademark lousy bedside manner. It was Doc's doctrine that he put everything he had into curing folks, didn't have anything left over for small talk or hand-holding.

But the man was quite prepared to discuss Jordan Everson with his son. He considered his illness serious even though he'd failed to diagnose it. Stomach tumour was a possibility, as were about another half-dozen ailments which could be suggested by the symptoms. He reminded Duane that his father had always been a difficult and headstrong patient who didn't really trust physicians and in recent times had displayed a regrettable enthusiasm for other sorts of medicine which he received from his housekeeper, the handsome but distant Mrs Janet Barker.

No. He could not suggest any form of treatment as he had not been given the chance to make a positive diagnosis. In response to Duane's query he grudgingly conceded that the housekeeper and the twins appeared to be affording his father excellent care. But in the absence of diagnosis and specific treatment he couldn't see Jordan improving on laudanum and 'quasi-medical gobbledygook' of which he claimed the housekeeper to be an exponent.

'You know how bad things have got out there with your daddy so scared of dying he won't listen to me any more, young Everson? The closest thing to medical qualifications that housekeeper's got is that her husband's an apothecary over in Harmonica, but that's enough for Jordan. He's got her dosing him up on God alone knows what, I had one too many quarrels with him about it and he threw me out. B'God, that man's been bull-headed and eccentric all his life, but he was never plumb loco before. You'll have to do something now you're back, laddy buck. Do something before it's too late. Now, Jana, will you send in Mrs Clacker on your way out. Would you believe she's got the shingles again? Third time this spring!'

It was mid afternoon when they quit the surgery. The couple strolled down the street in easy conversation and it was not until they drew up before the familiar clapboard building set back off the street with maples growing in the yard that Duane realized his companion had led him deliberately to the school.

'Come on,' she said in her bossy way, tugging his sleeve. 'Miss Hollitt would skewer me if she knew we'd passed right by her door without so much as a *buenos dias*.'

'Damnit, I've got to see the sheriff.'

She put a fingertip to the frown-crease between his eyes.

'You are still so serious about everything, *campañero*. Did you know I always used to wonder why you never smiled while Jesse never seemed to stop?' Then she grabbed him by the hand and pulled. '*Vamos*, we go. No?'

Soon Duane found himself seated in the schoolmistress's office with silver-haired Miss Hollitt keenly studying him across her desk, and Jana at his side, smiling behind her hands. He'd forgotten just what a tough old biddy this schoolmarm had always been.

He was soon on the griddle.

'Well, young man, at least you appear to have graduated into man's estate rather successfully, which is more than I can say for many of my pupils. How is your father?'

'He's been better.'

'He's been better, who?'

He shot a hard look at Jana. What the devil was he doing here when he had so many pressing matters to attend to anyway?

'Ma'am,' he added grudgingly.

'That's better. And what brought you back after you left so intemperately, might I ask?'

'I have my reasons.'

Miss Hollitt studied him through her pince-nez.

'Still reserved, stubborn and possibly solitary, so I see. Hmm, interesting. You always displayed ability at subjects you enjoyed, yet I recall your independent streak tended to isolate you. Would you consider that a fair assessment of your younger persona, Duane Everson?'

'Maybe.'

'You were always different.'

'Tell me something I don't know. Er, ma'am.'

Jana kicked him under the desk. He ignored it. Miss Hollitt appeared a little peeved.

'You and your brother were always such a contrast. He was talkative, sociable but poor scholastically. You on the other hand were quiet and reserved yet you worked very hard.'

'I had to. Jesse was smarter.'

'Quicker perhaps. There's a difference. But then your brother was never half the horseman you were, as I recall.'

'I'm good enough at what I do. But I'm a realist too. Jesse got Jordan's talents.'

'Why did you always feel you had to defend your older brother, Duane?'

He scowled. 'I don't do that.'

Miss Hollitt smiled sweetly. 'You're doing it now. Ingrained habits of childhood are so difficult to change, aren't they? Take Jana for instance. Prettiest girl I ever taught, but oh, what a difficult pupil! No discipline, precocious for her years and just riddled with old-world Spanish melancholy and cynicism at such a tender age. Tsk, tsk. And when I see her promenading down the main street in garments barely adequate to cover her decency, I only wish I'd been more generous with the birch. But I'm sure you're not hearing anything from me you've not heard a hundred times before, are you, Jana dear?'

This improved Duane's mood some and they quit the schoolhouse soon afterwards to head back for Pioneer Street. Jana, unfazed by the teacher's comments about herself, wanted what she termed a sundowner, meaning a tall glass containing a large amount of rye whiskey and very little water. But the day was running short of hours and he still had to see the sheriff, he explained.

She accepted this with good grace, chucking him under the chin and extracting a promise he would come see her again 'Before traipsing off to Arizona or Africa,' as she put it. '*Adios, hombrecito.*'

He stood before the apothecary's, watching her make her way along the walk, still as uninhibited as a schoolgirl yet there was certainly nothing childish about the way she looked.

He sighed. Jana had diverted him from other matters and he was grateful for it. But he had refocused on them by the time he reached the jailhouse which stood between the bank his father part-owned and the three-storeyed offices of the Montana Lumber Company which Jordan owned lock, stock and barrel.

Sheriff Buck Tune was a short man, built thick and solid with strong shoulders. He sported a greying moustache and had sharp brown eyes. Duane figured he was about forty but looked more like fifty. His was a wide area of jurisdiction peopled in part by brawling lumberjacks, gold-crazy miners, contrary Indians and cold-eyed men with tied-down revolvers. He took his duties seriously and was well regarded. Duane came to him looking for straight answers and got what he was looking for, but only up to a point.

In the light of yesterday's shooting incident at Suspicion Canyon the lawman was now ready to believe Jordan, who kept insisting someone was out to kill him. His deputies were still out combing the hills for the gunman involved but hopes of success were rapidly fading.

Naturally Tune was concerned about Duane's father's illness, but he also expressed alarm regarding the gunmen Cloud Valley now had on its payroll, fearing their presence could increase tensions and possibly, in time, pose a challenge to law and order.

'You should know, young Duane, that this here attempt on your life doesn't surprise me too much. All things considered, that is.'

'Better explain that, Sheriff.'

The lawman sighed, leaned back.

'This county's gone downhill fast ever since your father took sick; that's the long and the short of things. As you'd know better than most, Jordan employs more men, heads up more companies and exerts more political muscle than any ten men. He's the engine that drives Bear Lake County, and ever since that engine started faltering I've been watching things going to hell in a handbasket here.'

'Meaning?'

'Meaning his business rivals and enemies are getting pushier and cockier by the day. Your father's got more enemies than my hound's got fleas, and you can believe they've been flexing their muscles with him out of the picture. Suddenly there's sharp deals being hatched, snaky-looking strangers hanging about and more trouble in the saloons for me and my deputies to deal with. There's been a big upsurge in rustlings and outlawry in the boondocks, and badmen and riff-raff keep drifting our way from Canada and the Dakotas faster than we can keep tabs. And all on account of the strong hand's not on the tiller any more. You savvy, son?'

He nodded. He appreciated the badge-toter's confidence. But he wanted to know more. Certainly he was interested in county affairs. But when it came right down to cases, Cloud Valley was his real concern.

'What exactly do you know about what's going on out at the ranch, Sheriff?' he asked bluntly, and suddenly Buck Tune seemed distracted by a fly crawling up his window pane.

'Nothing I could put my finger on, young Duane,' he declared vaguely. He took a swipe at the fly with a rolled-up newspaper, missed by a mile. 'Of course I'm hoping things will improve now you're back. I'm not saying your kid brother isn't taking best care he can of your daddy on account of I'm sure he is. But Tyran, well, in my opinion he spends far too much time around town, has far too much money to spend and might even choose his company a little careless-like. You get my drift?'

Duane wasn't sure he did. He attempted to draw the man out further, but that was as much as Buck Tune was prepared to offer. He proved close-lipped on the subject of the influential housekeeper but managed to convey the impression that he felt the woman had more authority and influence over the twins than perhaps was appropriate.

Trouble was, Tyran and Beth worried Duane not a little himself. Just today, Miss Hollitt had assessed him as somewhat solitary and self-contained as a pupil. He felt Tyran and Beth shared similar charac-teristics. They plainly preferred one another's company – along with that of the housekeeper, of course. As Tune intimated, they were often in town where Tyran had developed a reputation as a drinker, gambler and saloon-lizard.

He was considering these matters as he rose to leave. Then Tune hit him with the question he guessed he should have anticipated.

'What brought you home, Duane?'

'You should know, Sheriff,' he answered as they stepped out onto the porch. 'It was you who told me he was sick.'

'So, that was enough to bring you all the way from Arizona?'

Duane watched the lamplighter go by on his flatbed wagon, touching flame to the Rager lamps with a long-handled taper-holder. Night was falling and a chill was in the air. Twilight. The beginning of nothing to do.

'You'd have to concede that in light of what

happened yesterday it might be just as well I am back, Sheriff.'

'I'm glad you are. We all are. But it still seems a big step for you to take, considering the way you left and all. . . .'

Duane just nodded and went on his way. He knew exactly the reason he'd elected to return home but hadn't revealed it to anybody. Most likely he never would.

4

Blood Kin

The side door opened and a step sounded in the entranceway, and then brisk footsteps coming down the unlit hall. Turk came into the back room and glanced first at the sweating croupier leaning against the wall, then cut his stare to the calm-faced man seated in a tipped-back chair behind the desk with hands linked behind his neck, who greeted him with a soft:

'So?'

Gray Leonard was a smooth man with a voice and manner ideally suited to his profession. People who visited his Domino gambling hall in Doubletree were both impressed and reassured by the cultivated voice and manner. They were so taken in by his easy charm they couldn't wait to try and take advantage of such a pleasant gentleman by running white-hot at poker or roulette and hurling him into bankruptcy. Many had tried but Gray Leonard was still highly solvent. He was far harder than he looked and made a point of never overlooking the little things.

Turk, late of Cloud Valley, dipped into his pocket and drew out a small drawstring canvas bag which clunked heavily when dropped on the desk.

'One hundred and fifty bucks in one dollars, Mr Leonard,' he reported, flicking his eyes at the shining-faced croupier. 'It was under his bed.'

'What a coincidence, wouldn't you say, Tucker?' Leonard purred. 'Our books come up shy one-fifty, we find one-fifty, under your bed.'

With a choked-off gasp of fear, the croupier made a frantic rush for the passageway. He didn't make it. A big boot tripped him and as he went down Turk's fist slammed the back of his neck. His face struck the floor and blood flowed. Turk shot a glance at the man behind the desk. He nodded. Turk allowed Tucker to struggle to his feet then seized his frilled shirtfront in his left hand, screwed it tight and then commenced slapping his face from side to side with a slow brutal rhythm. The savagery continued for a full minute with Leonard watching impassively and Turk enjoying his work, when another footfall sounded outside in the darkened hallway. Immediately Leonard dropped his chair legs to the floor and went to the door to see a dim figure standing there in the gloom.

'That will be all for now, Turk,' he said and the big man went out the second door dragging the unconscious dealer behind him like a bag of dirt. Leonard put on his table-captain's smile and turned back to the passageway.

'Do come in, Tyran. So pleased you could make it.'

The hour between six and seven is the quiet hour upon the street. It is then that the blackjack dealers from the Domino gambling hall and the piano-players from the Deacon Bench, the Cattle Queen and Fat Maisie's take their supper, then sit smoking and enjoying the cool air on the porches and galleries before the rush. Shutters are drawn tight at the Boman Everson Bank and the president is across the street at the Queen sipping blended bourbon while his underpaid clerks work on. Gray Leonard emerges from his plush rooms at the hotel and, with flunkies in attendance, commences his nightly promenade down the main stem to Chicken Pickles' eatery - best chow in town, passing Drunk Tank Johnny without a glance. There'll be no clam chowder awaiting Drunk Tank at his packing-crate home in back of the general store, just an old dog to greet him, sniffing at his pockets to see if he's brought any liver.

Then the piano begins to tinkle at the Poker Chip Palace and shortly draws answering music from the Cattle Queen across the street and two doors down. Eateries empty, someone kicks a dog, boardwalks begin to stutter to the drum of cowboy boots and high-heeled dancing-shoes.

Doubletree's night is under way.

Duane was shaking hands with a couple of old school buddies he'd met by chance and dined with at the hotel, just as the town-hall clock chimed seven. Pot roast and apple pie washed down with a jug of pale beer shared with good company had set him up for the ride home. The shootout at the canyon and the tensions back on the Valley had drifted into the background over the past couple of hours. But it was high time to be heading back and he was making off for the livery when the tinny sound of a bugle sounded somewhere up the street, warning that the stage was coming in.

The mud-spattered Concord drawn by six mustang mules overtook him half a block from the stage depot. He barely spared the rig a glance as he set a freshly rolled Durham between his teeth and felt his pockets for matches. He was feeling good. The day behind him had afforded an opportunity to take a more detached look at situations and events. There were still many things he had to look into and analyse, while there was no denying that whoever it was who'd made an attempt on his life was still out there someplace with a gun. And Jordan was still Jordan; nothing could change that.

He almost grinned as he propped to light up. He could handle the old man, he believed. The first objective he must tackle was to somehow persuade him to consult a bona fide doctor and find out just what his illness was, then set about curing it. He was sure he could do that. Things were moving and he was making them move, and right now he wasn't missing the relaxed Arizonan lifestyle and its unstressed pace one little bit.

They were offloading the stage as he drew abreast of the landing. As he glanced across a tall man was descending the steps with his head turned away, speaking to someone alighting behind. The passenger had wide shoulders, a small waist and long lean legs. He wore a tailored suit and double gunrig, thick fair hair curled long over the collar of his coat beneath a rakish hat.

Duane propped in his tracks, feeling a tingle along his spine as he realized how familiar that athletic shape appeared. Then the passenger turned his head to laugh at something a porter said, and the landing-lights fell full upon his face.

Jesse!

'How's she doin' now, Duane?'

'Improving,' grunted Duane, making a final adjustment to the strapping he'd placed on the white filly's off foreleg. He uncoiled to his feet with the the stable lantern throwing his shadow across the yellow straw. The filly was starting to eat, a good sign. 'Tell the wrangler I'll keep her here overnight where I can keep an eye on her. If she's OK in the morning she can go back to the pasture.'

The bow-legged hand nodded his close-cropped head.

'You sure got a touch with hosses. I thought she might've been done for, the way she was limpin' when the herd came in.'

Duane wiped his hands on a cotton swab.

'They drove them down too fast from the top forty. You've got to take it easy when you mix young stuff with rough trails.'

The man grinned.

'As you let them boys know in no uncertain way, huh, Duane? You gave them waddies a real chewin' out, so they tell me.' The man paused a moment as the sounds of laughter reached the stables from the house. 'Great day, will you listen to that. How long since anyone heard laughin' round here, I wonder. Mister, I never met you or your brother until last week, but that Jesse's sure made a heap of difference hereabouts, ain't he?'

'A heap. Don't you have chores to tend?'

'Chores at night? Hey, we're not all work and no play hotshots like you, Mr Duane, nosiree.'

'I told you to check the mares they brought down to see if they needed blanketing. Did you do it?'

The man coloured. 'Guess I clean forgot. I mean, after supper Jesse came over and started tellin' us about them women in Jasper and I guess—'

'Do it now.'

'Whatever you say, boss!' he flared and flung from the stables in a snit. 'What a sorehead!' he muttered, but loud enough for his voice to carry back. 'Likely just ornery on account big brother's come back and stole his thunder iffen you ask me. . . .'

His words faded. Duane's expression didn't change as he slung his denim jacket over his shoulder and took the passageway between the stalls through to the front.

There was still laughter and loud talk across at the house. Busying his fingers with tobacco and papers, he leaned the point of his shoulder against the doorframe and counted heads round the table on the front gallery. Only two left now, Jesse and his father. No sign of the twins, nor the housekeeper for that matter. It was late for Jordan to be outdoors in light clothing and he heard him cough as Jesse reached out to refill his glass. Then he laughed again, and Duane had to concede the ranch hand had likely been right just now. Who'd laughed around Cloud Valley until a couple of days ago?

He lit up and drew deep.

He didn't feel at all put out but could understand others thinking he might be. In truth he was damned glad Jesse had dropped like a bolt from the blue the way he had. It was great to have him around, as always. And Jordan was like a new man even if all the excitement was exhausting him. Duane felt revitalized himself. Growing up together, the very different brothers had always hit it off just fine even if he had grown up with the tag of 'Jesse's shadow'.

He'd envied his brother back then. But not any longer. Jesse could fight, shoot, dance, play poker, skip rocks, spark girls and light up a room just about better than anyone he'd ever known. It had been easy for his kid brother just to seem to tag along with whatever he wanted to do because he did so many things so well. But they were both grown men now and Duane's life was just how he wanted it, had been ever since that epic day eight years ago when he'd grabbed destiny by the horns and opted out of a life he no longer wanted.

Freedom had topped his wish list after seventeen years in Montana. Freedom to work at what he was good at – horses – and the peace of mind that came with being his own man and stepping out of the shadow of two dominating personalities.

It had been tough saying goodbye to his brother, but easy bidding the old man *adios*. He doubted if Jordan had even noticed him gone. For he'd still had Jesse, at least for a while, and they were more like brothers than father and son. Small wonder Tyran seemed to have grown up with all sorts of twists and kinks to his character. After the twins' mother opted out of the marriage and went to live in Boston, Jordan seemed to pay that boy no attention at all.

And he thought as he drew on his smoke: Tyran should have quit like I did. He might well have found a new and better life for himself. Like me.

Freedom and independence topped his wish list at

seventeen years of age. He found both in Black Mesa County, Southern Arizona, where he quickly built up a reputation with the big horse outfits, thus guaranteeing a healthy income which in time enabled him to set himself up on his own piece of land where he began hunting and breaking the wild mustangs of the deserts and plains. Within a year he was doing well enough to be able to work when he liked and play whenever it took his fancy. Hunting, fishing or just simply drifting through the Indian country either alone or with friends. Chasing a maverick herd of wild mustangs across forty miles of sunbaked plain; carousing nightlong in bordertown saloons; women, but not yet any particular woman; floating alone down the muddy Chino River searching for the spot where Coronado had crossed in his quest for the Seven Cities of Gold.

Whenever he tired of that it was back to the Alameda and the routine. Coffee at first light, then into the corrals to deal with the first of the long line of vicious tempered 'unbreakables' his crew had snared during his absence.

A meaningful life. No skyrocket highs, maybe. But no dark Montana gloomdays either. And virtually total freedom from secrecy, vanity, arrogance, wealth and contorted family ties.

It was the way a man should live and had a right to expect. And it might have gone on for ever but for a brief report in his subscription copy of the Montanan newspaper that afforded the first hint that Jordan might be ill.

'Hey, what you doing, Bro?'

Tyran had come up behind him through the stables, the horse noises blotting his footsteps. The

waft of wine hit Duane in the face. His brother was
weaving on his fancy high-heel boots. For once, there
was no sign of Beth.

'Party winding down?' Duane asked.

'Some party!' Tyran rammed his hands into his
pants pockets and squinted across at the house. ' So
where's he going to sleep?'

'Huh? Who?'

'Big brother, of course. Jesse the almighty. No way
known he's going to be able to drag that great
swelled head of his in through daddy's doorjambs.
He might have to bed down on the meadow.'

A faint smile creased Duane's cheeks. 'All right,
kid, what's Jesse been saying that's got you sore?'

Tyran Everson sniffed. The young man had
acquired a whole showcase of strange personal habits
over the years. He stared across the ranchyard at the
house, refusing to meet Duane's eyes, fidgeting with
the watch-chain slung across his striped vest.

'Don't quite know how to say this, Duane.'

'Whatever it is, try saying it straight.'

The young man scuffed his fancy boots and
rubbed the back of his neck.

'It's just that I think maybe it would be best if you
and Jesse left.' Now he looked up sharply. 'Nothing
personal, you understand. But the truth is Jordan was
doing better before you fellows came back. You seem
to upset him, which is bad, and Jesse excites him,
which is even worse. Hope you don't mind my being
honest with you, but that's just how I see it. So, er . . .
what do you say?'

'Before I say anything maybe you'd like to tell me
how your luck is running.'

'How's that?'

'You've got quite a reputation in town as a gambling man. Matter of fact I hear that lately some of the big poker games you've been involved in at Leonard's have drawn crowds. Riding a streak, are you?'

'Born lucky and good looking, Bro,' Tyran quipped, only his smile was forced. 'But let's get back to you and Jesse. You were looking pretty good here until he showed, wouldn't you agree? I mean, the old man was cheered to have you back even if he didn't show it. You bucked everyone up, even Sis and me on account you've got a kind of way about you that calms folks down. But let's face it. Jesse showing out of the blue's set you right back to where you used to be in the old days, right? I mean, he was here five minutes and he had everyone eating out of the palm of his hand. I never hit it off with him but I'll be first to say he's a natural number one guy, Jordan all over again.' He paused. 'You paying attention, Rider?'

Duane frowned. He was concentrating, but not on what was being said. The stabled horses were acting restless. He both heard it and sensed it. Without a word he strode past Tyran's reaching grasp hand and made the corner in the passageway just in time to glimpse two billowing skirts vanish through the doorway leading out to the water-tank. He didn't need to see the women to know who they were. He rested hands on hips as a panting Tyran came rushing up, eyes wide and guilty-looking.

'Let me guess, kid,' Duane said quietly. 'You were put up to make that little speech, weren't you? So why do Beth and the housekeeper want us gone? Or maybe all three of you feel the same way?'

Tyran let out a hiss of either anger or frustration

and bolted off to to follow the women outside, leaving the door swinging slowly to stillness behind him on leather hinges. Joker rolled the yellow blob of his eye at Duane when he moved slowly across to his stall and leaned upon the half door.

'Ever get the yen to be back in Arizona, hoss? Right now I wouldn't blame you if you did.'

The horse nudged his elbow. It wanted oats.

5

Rough Night in Doubletree

The Everson brothers were holding court.

It was two days later, and with their father once again slipping away into a fog of pain and depression, both Duane and Jesse had ridden down to Doubletree to visit with Doc Greenlease and see if they couldn't persuade the crochety old medico to put his pride in his pocket, pack his fat black bag and return to the spread with them.

But the doc was out of town helping bring another mint-new Bear Lake County citizen into the world, and to ensure the day wasn't completely wasted, Jesse proposed a cleansing ale at the Cattle Queen before heading back.

That was three hours ago. The sun was well over both the yard-arm and the Civil War memorial sundial at the junction of Pioneer and Placer Streets now, and neither Everson was showing any inclination to make for the livery.

Jesse sat in the slanting sunlight at the top of the
steps leading up out of the ankle-deep dust of
Pioneer Street. He appeared totally at ease in the
saloon-keeper's personal easy-chair from his private
quarters upstairs from the roughest barroom in
town.

Mine host at the Queen was not generous or
hospitable by nature. He was a sour swag-bellied cuss
with a belt that would have gone round a horse, who
waddled instead of walked and was in trouble with
the sheriff on a regular basis for watering every item
on his shelves from sarsaparilla to his five-bucks-a-
bottle Tennessee whiskey.

Yet he couldn't do enough for the brothers for the
simple reason that, within half an hour of their
arrival, they were attracting customers like blow-flies
at a rib-roast.

It had always been that way when Jesse Everson was
around. He had the reputation of being able to turn
the saddest wake into the best wing-ding you'd ever
seen, just because he had that sort of style and
personality. Had had it as a nineteen-year-old when
he quit the county and his eight years away only
seemed to have burnished his almost universal
appeal.

Almost.

He didn't impress the swag-bellied saloon-
keeper, for instance. The man hated his flashy
looks and the fact that his father was the richest
man in a hundred miles. But as the fat mine host
hustled out now with a box of cigars for 'Two fine
fellers we've all been missin' somethin' fierce,'
Jesse and Duane were his best buddies. The cash
register inside on the dark and sagging bar hadn't

stopped ringing since morning, and now he saw
even the sheriff and judge wandering over from the
courthouse to swell the crowd.

'Where's your glass, old buddy?' he beamed at
Duane, perched on a corner of the gallery railing
some distance back from the steps. 'I'll send you out
another rye and chaser.'

'I'm fine for the moment – old buddy.'

The man vanished inside, shaking his head
worriedly. He feared that if Duane wasn't enjoying
himself the brothers might decided to go someplace
else and take everybody with them.

There was no chance of that. It was true that
Duane was well and truly in the background, chatting
idly to the odd citizen he'd worked with or attended
school with in the far past, smoking the odd Bull
Durham. But looks can be deceiving. He was having
one hell of a fine time. He always had done with his
Jesse.

He cocked his ear to listen as his brother finished
off one of his jokes:

' "So where's your sense of humour," this guy
asked his wife. "I lost it the day I carried you over the
threshold," she said.'

Everyone laughed, the girls from Maisie's, the trav-
eller in bob-wire, who was getting tipsy, the miners
from the Sister Fan and assorted blackjack dealers
and croupiers taking their ease before starting the
afternoon hitch at the Deacon Bench and the
Domino's rooms.

Jesse sipped his whiskey and crossed one booted
foot over his knee. He'd worn a stylish suit into town
but had discarded the jacket, which now hung on a
nail in a roof-support at his elbow. He wore a brocade

vest over a white linen shirt a housemaid had ironed
for him that morning, and one of the girls was wearing his hat with the throat-strap drawn up tightly
beneath her pretty chin. He rocked, puffed on a
courtesy cigar and allowed someone else to pick up
the conversational ball as he paused to watch life in
Doubletree flow by.

This time of the afternoon there was always a
bustle of traffic on the main stem, horsemen, wagons
and people on foot, the shoppers and traders and
those looking for business and those just out to
squeeze as much out of the day as possible, like
himself.

In the thick shadow of the arcade opposite, a knot
of out-of-work lumberjacks were standing talking and
occasionally glancing over at the Cattle Queen.
These men were unemployed for the simple reason
they'd been working for the wrong lumber outfit,
which had eventually been forced to shut down
operations. This was directly due to the fact that the
Everson Lumber Company had acquired the supply
contracts their outfit had with the Monarch Railroad
and was now supplying all their needs from
Drumgriff Basin.

Sick or well, Jordan always came up out on top
whether it be in commerce, politics or even with
women. Maybe especially with women.

Jesse grinned at this thought as he lifted his glass.
He was a handsome male animal with husky shoulders and hair the colour of a cornfield. True, there
were some lines that hard living had etched in his
tanned features over his years away. But the eyes were
the same powder-blue people remembered and his
natural charm seemed even more assured and

potent than ever.

Of course you couldn't be stylish, handsome and the son of a rich man without making enemies, human nature being what it was. He'd been criticized for being superficial, vain, immoral and more than a tad work-shy and not always choosy about whom he drank or slept with.

The girls from Maisie's had never met him before today but were of one mind that he was by far the most dynamic stud to come riding by since Maisie set up shop. One of them was perched on his knee when the sheriff and judge drew up at the foot of the steps.

'Some people have it easy,' Buck Tune grinned. 'You realize you boys are causing an obstruction here, I suppose?'

'Arrest us and I'll tell everybody about the judge and Fast Kitty Devine, Sheriff,' Jesse fired back, and everyone laughed, including the judge. The judge was on two of Jordan Everson's boards, while Jordan's political support ensured Buck Tune got voted back every year regular as the sunrise.

The new arrivals allowed Duane to treat them to a drink but didn't venture up onto the gallery for fear of compromising themselves in the eyes of the conservative element in the electorate. Doubletree was that kind of town, vigorous and prosperous but largely law-abiding and correct, thanks mainly to sheriff and judge.

They wanted to keep their town that way, which was why both men were concerned about recent events at Valley Ranch. They might have liked to discuss some of these matters with the brothers today but plainly it was not the right time. They eventually left and their places were almost immediately taken by the county's perennial Pretender to Jordan Everson's King, Gray Leonard.

The entrepreneur, wheeler-dealer and owner of the Domino gambling hall had come a long way in eight years, the brothers were aware. Back then he'd been just a dealer at the Deacon Bench trying to put enough together to take up a quarter section along the Red Warrior south of town.

Today Leonard wore a diamond stickpin in his cravat and came accompanied by three hard faced 'assistants', as he called them, one of them the former Cloud Valley bodyguard, Turk, still showing visible signs of his brush with Duane and his horse.

'Is this a private party or can anyone join in?' the new arrival asked with a smooth smile, touching fingers to the brim of his grey fedora. 'Jesse, Duane, nice to see you fellows back in the county at a time when your father needs you. Might I buy you a drink?'

'Sorry, we were just on our way,' Jesse said, uncoiling to his feet and taking down his jacket. 'Another time, maybe, eh, Duane?'

'Sure, when we're not so busy,' Duane affirmed, coming down the steps. For a moment it seemed as if Turk would block his way. But Leonard said something and the hard man moved aside. With his coat over his shoulder, Jesse joined him and the brothers stood together as the town remembered them, tall Jesse and the quiet Rider with his horseman's build and walk. Leonard seemed about to move on but paused, looking from one to the other.

'I might as well be frank, boys. When I heard you were in town I decided I had to talk with you.'

'About what?' asked Duane.

'You know about my bid for the South Basin

timber rights through the Company?' Duane nodded and the man went on. 'Fellers, Drumgriff's got the best lumber in five hundred miles, and I could sell a mess of it if I could get hold of that lease. Well, my bid's been before your father's board for six weeks but I haven't had a response. I guess that's because of his health but I certainly would appreciate it if you could, like, jog his memory for him and maybe put in a good word. For old time's sake, huh?'

Duane shrugged and Jesse murmured, "Yeah, well, OK.' Jordan had never really involved them in the big-business side of his operations. They'd been too young before they left, and the topic had not arisen since their return.

'I'd be real obliged. So why not stop by my place later?' Leonard invited, looking from face to face in a strangely intense way. 'Lots of action at the Domino. Isn't that right, Turk?'

'Right,' Turk grunted, fingering his healing mouth. 'See you there,' he added darkly to Duane.

'Sore loser?' Jesse speculated as the party moved on.

'He's just small potatoes,' was Duane's comment. 'But Leonard has sure spread his wings. They tell me he now owns Charity Creek Ranch, and he's been making bids to buy into Drumgriff all year. Must be successful, I guess. I'd figure timber rights to South Basin would cost big bucks.'

'Well, he always was a kind of hustling, hungry pilgrim in a big hurry to get somewhere as I recall. Well, where to now?'

'I thought you had someplace to go?'

Jesse laughed as he set his hat on the back of his head. 'Hell no.' He waved a cheery goodbye to the crowd on the gallery. 'Just need a change of scenery.'

'Same old Jesse. Always need to be moving on.'

The taller man threw an arm around his brother's shoulders. 'And same old Rider. You just can't wait until we've got the old man back on his feet so you can get back to your ranch and likely stay right there in the one place, happy as a puppy on a warm brick. Can you?'

'Maybe.' There was no maybe about it. Jesse was reading him like large print. 'Does it show?'

'You got the South in your blood,' Jesse said, sober for a moment as he surveyed the streetscape. 'Just like Ma. She came from there and never really left it, in her head. And you and Ma were even more of a piece than the old man and me.'

His brother never said a truer word.

Jesse punched his shoulder.

'C'mon, it's chow time. We'll put ourselves outside some vittles then see what trouble we can scare up down Rooney Street.'

'You think that's a good idea?' Duane asked as they started across the street. 'It's still rough as old hay-bales down there, so they tell me. They'd still rather fight than eat, that's when they're not climbing into bed with their best friends' women.'

'You make it sound even better than I recall. Let's hustle.'

They quickly discovered that the Hot Skillet still cooked the best steak in town. They shared a table with the owner and his wife who'd both attended Doubletree School with them. The couple brought them up to date on the latest gossip as they worked through the blue-plate special: sirloin, mashed potatoes, three varieties of beans and a slab of apple pie while a sweet little Greek with a huge black moustache and an eight-string guitar strummed melodies from the Old Country, pausing now and then to brush a sentimental tear from the eye.

It was no accident that they steered the conversation round to Cloud Valley and the testing times that had befallen their father. The brothers now accepted that Jordan was a sick man, possibly had even contracted something potentially fatal. But there were other aspects of the situation on the spread that had bothered Duane and now seemed to be having the same effect upon Jesse.

The whole unsatisfactory business of Doc Greenlease's dismissal, and the formidable housekeeper's assumption of responsibility for Jordan's care was their major concern, and nothing the couple said about the situation seemed in any way reassuring.

'That Janet Barker seems to have a whole lot of pull out there, so we hear,' said the wife. 'According to Doc Greenlease, she was behind your dad getting rid of him. And it seems Tyran and Beth do pretty much whatever she says too. Does this worry you boys?'

They had to admit it did, some. But taking the time to kick the subject around, which they hadn't had the opportunity to do since Jesse's return, they had to agree that Mrs Barker ran the house very well, and that regardless of what their feelings might be, Jordan's confidence in her was strong. And this being the case, it was taken as understood that there didn't seem to be much they could do about the situation at the moment other than just go along with it.

The topic switched to Duane's shootout at

Suspicion Canyon. Their friends informed them that the violent episode had been the prime topic of gossip round town, and people were getting nervous. There was a feeling abroad now that there might well be substance in Jordan's allegations about attempts upon his life. The brothers learned that there was a new tough element in town these days, some of whom comprised Jordan's own protection force, but there were also others of the same stripe who observed strange hours and kept their noses relatively clean, but made folks edgy just the same.

They had plenty to occupy their minds when they quit the eatery and headed south in the late afternoon. But their serious mood only lasted as long as it took to turn out of Pioneer three blocks down and swing past Quality Buffalo Meats to find themselves once again on Rooney Street.

It looked just as they remembered, grimy, down at heel and no place for a respectable person to find himself at mid morning, much less coming on towards dusk. With a saloon on every corner, Rooney Street was for any man with nothing left to lose.

Or perhaps for a pair of brothers who'd been sneaking down here since they first graduated to long pants, and therefore had a working idea of where to go to have most fun, and where not to show your face after dark.

It was amazing how fast time could fly at the old no-name dive across from the pig butcher's where whiskey was just a dime a shot and, by a stroke of coincidence, the poetic guitar player from the eatery worked nights.

They still knew enough people down here to

almost guarantee their safety, and as for all the surly unwashed others, Jesse's talent for making friends and squeezing a night out until it hollered saw them eventually accepted – and the night picked up its tempo from there on in. Soon everyone was dancing to the music of the soulful guitarist, and Jesse was first up and last to sit down. Duane enjoyed himself to the hilt but in his own different way. The big feature of the night for him was the realization that he and his brother had needed this time together to paper over the inevitable gaps in their relationship that were the simple result of eight years apart.

Duane was discussing horses with a stove-up rodeo rider shortly before midnight when he felt a tap on his shoulder.

''Allo, Rider.'

Jana Castillo's voluptuous curves were hidden beneath a shapeless hip-length coat worn against the night's chill. She smiled at Duane's obvious surprise and introduced him to her companion, a buxom woman sporting a splendid black eye. The woman had been injured by a drunken husband, went to Doc Greenlease late at night for treatment, learned he was out of town, and knocked up Jana instead. They'd been passing the dive when the rare sight of two respectable-looking clients caught Jana's eye and she recognized them both.

For the next two hours they were a foursome, with Jesse flirting outrageously with Jana without making much apparent headway and Duane discovering that the shabby woman with the shiner danced like a dream. But not, of course, as well as Jana. And both brothers were wide-eyed with wonder when the drinkers finally persuaded Jana to shuck her coat and jump up on a table to dance to the guitarist's smoking version of 'The Mexican Hat Dance' and 'Johnny in The Low Ground'.

Then it was time for the whole well-oiled gathering to grow emotional and join in the choruses of 'She Wore a Wreath of Roses' and 'Long Long Ago'. This had all the makings of a memorable night.

'Tell me about it one more time, Rider. *Por favor?*'

'About what?'

'The *rancho*, of course. And the wind, and how you say it comes at night like a lover and brings the smells of Old Mexico . . .'

'Did I say all that?'

'Do not tease . . . tell me. . . .'

He did as he was asked. Speaking eloquently about his horse ranch by the river with Black Mesa in the distance and the trail from Tucson running by his door, was as easy as sipping sourmash for the man from the South. So he described how the Santa Ana winds could conjure up images of a million sizzling *frijoles* and sultry *señoritas* waiting for the night and lovers. How wild mustangs he'd completely broken to saddle and bridle could sniff these breezes and grow wild and restless again and sometimes bust loose on a summer midnight to run, run, run for the simple ecstasy of being alive, and how sometimes he would just let them go. For the same spirit that stirred their blood pulsed in his veins also.

Then he almost blushed as he realized that bad booze and good company seemed to have stampeded his tongue.

But Jana loved it and wanted more. Instead he said:

'How come you never went back South? We always talked about it. It was what you said, and it was the stories Ma told me of Arizona that first made me realize I'd never belonged here in the North and never would. Why, Jana?'

'I had no one to go to. Better here as an outsider than down South amongst strangers.'

This was getting too deep for him.

'Let's hear Red River Valley!' he shouted to their own private guitar virtuoso. He swept the girl to her feet, and they joined Jesse on the little dancefloor with the woman with the black eye whose ugly husband would soon show up and start a fight.

Midnight had come and gone when Jana and the Eversons walked the woman home to her shack, after which the trio strode arm in arm back up Rooney and into Pioneer like people without a care in the world and feeling little pain.

But ingrained habits die hard. With the girl's arm tucked through his and Jesse executing a strange little tap-hop every few paces as they approached the darkened alleymouth, Duane was not consciously looking for anything untoward, but sensed it nonetheless.

A rat scuttled from the alley into the light, and instinct told him the critter wouldn't do that unless something scared it. Well aware they were still on the rougher side of town, he untucked his arm and stepped quickly forward to peer into the alleyway just as the man lurking there ducked out of it some thirty yards down.

He would have let it go at that but for the fact that he was next door to certain that the slim silhouette of the nightowl was Tyran's.

What the hell was the kid doing in Doubletree this time of night when they'd left him in charge of their father?

He alerted the others and they gave chase, liquor fumes dissipating fast as the brothers led Jana round the corner and set off in pursuit of the fast-running figure down an unlighted street which went twisting back towards the centre of town.

'Tyran!' Jesse roared. 'Wait up. It's us!'

The effect of this was to see the boy clap on speed. He was beginning to draw away from them when he suddenly swerved out of sight round the blacksmith's corner. He was cutting across a vacant lot in back of the sprawl of the Domino gambling hall when they brought him in sight again.

It grew complicated from there. Ugly.

By the time the three were crossing the lot it was obvious the Domino was Tyran's objective. Again, they might have let it go at that had they not found his behaviour so mystifying and, yes, somehow offensive. Duane was in the lead by this time and he saw the boy's figure vanish up a set of stairs mere moments before a powerful silhouette detached from an outbuilding and moved swiftly to block their path.

'And just what do you nightowls think you're about?' the figure challenged. Duane slowed to a jog, then halted. For the second time in a week he found himself confronting big Turk in a tense situation.

'Step aside,' he panted. 'Our brother just went in there.'

'So?'

'So – step aside, you ape,' Jesse growled, and

swung. The punch caught the big man flush on the jaw and he sagged, going down on one side like a house with a collapsing pier. Turk fell to all fours, dazed and leaking blood. But before the brothers could make it to the stairs dark figures erupted from the doorway where Tyran had vanished.

There were three of them and they were not interested in discussion. They came down in full attack mode and the brothers met them head on.

The half-minute that followed was a test of mettle. The Domino doormen set the agenda, coming in hard with billy-clubs and boots, looking for a quick victory. They might have got it but for Jesse's pistoning fists. Duane's brother had been a college boxing champion and was built for fighting with his strength and lightning reflexes. He took a numbing blow to his left arm from a chopping club blow early in the mêlée but retaliated with a right hook which sent his attacker spinning towards Duane, who tripped him up then finished him off with a kick to the jaw as he went over.

Assessing Jesse as the main danger, the other two closed on his tall figure from opposite directions. But it was a mistake to overlook Duane, as they quickly learned. He might lack Jesse's size and power but was quick and clear-headed under fire. Coming up from behind the bigger of the two enforcers he sledged a forearm to the back of an unguarded neck. The man was driven forward onto Jesse's rip to the guts that had him jack-knifing and heaving his guts.

Suddenly outnumbered, the third man beat a retreat for the steps. Duane scooped up a dropped baton and hurled it with all his strength. There was a dull clunk of contact and the runner slewed sideways.

He cannoned into Turk just as he was getting to his feet. Both fell in a tangle and the grim-faced Eversons were closing in fast when suddenly Gray Leonard was there on the steps, hands upraised, smooth face white with shock.

'Boys, boys, no more, please! There's been a misunderstanding. Let me explain.'

'It had better be good, Leonard,' panted Jesse, massaging his arm and spitting blood.

'Real good,' Duane affirmed. His hand was on his gun-handle. He didn't trust Gray Leonard and saw no reason why he should.

6

The Sins of the Father

The back room was stark and austere in contrast to
the opulence of the Domino's gaming rooms.
Someone produced sandwiches and coffee but
nobody was hungry. Leonard had already invited
Jesse and Duane to occupy the chairs at the bare desk
but they remained standing. Although there was now
no sign of any Domino personnel, neither man felt
reassured and they remained alert and suspicious as
they listened to his explanations. Tyran sat miserably
in a far corner chewing his fingernails. Beyond the
misting window-panes the night was quiet.

The boy's over-concern for his father's health and
peace of mind – that was the simple truth of the
whole regrettable matter, so Leonard insisted in his
plausible way.

The brothers traded looks. It was crystal-clear by
this that the gambler and the kid were on close terms.
Just as it was coming clear to them that they didn't
have the right to come back and start finding faults

after all this time. Tyran was free to make his own friends even if they mightn't think too much of them.

They nodded and the gambler spread his hands.

'You see, gentlemen, it came to Tyran's ears tonight that his big brothers were in town and tying one on. Naturally he was concerned you might get drunk which would be upsetting for your dad, the condition he's in. So, sure, he tagged you down to Rooney Street, and was still keeping a brotherly eye on you boys on your way back to the central block when he was spotted.'

'So why did he bolt like a scared rabbit?' Jesse wanted to know, glancing across at Tyran, who refused to meet his eye.

There was another simple explanation for that. And the gambling boss had it.

Surely the brothers must know Tyran had been in serious trouble with his father concerning the time he spent off the ranch coupled with his spending and gambling? He'd simply slipped away from Cloud Valley last night and had hoped to return with nobody but his sister being any the wiser. Naturally he'd taken flight when they'd spotted him. Who wouldn't?

'And your plug-uglies jumping us?' Duane challenged. He'd never liked this man and was not warming to him any tonight. 'Thought we were bandits come to rob the place, maybe?'

Gray Leonard smiled tolerantly. 'Hardly, Duane. No, when the boy rushed in all het up and scared, my men just naturally thought he'd been set upon by hooligans. One of the drawbacks in being a rich man's son, I suppose. And speaking of rich men,' he said, turning very sober as he rose. 'Can we rely on you not to make mention of this to your father?'

'You mustn't tell Dad,' Tyran chimed in now, jumping up. He was white and sick-looking, they saw; the kid looked a mess. 'He's been happy since you both came home but something like this would really set him back. And he might even throw me out, who knows?'

Jesse looked at Duane, who looked hard at the youth. He was deeply suspicious about the whole episode, as indeed he was of this connection between Tyran and Leonard. He was a long way short of being sure he believed what they were being told, was still sore at the way the bruisers had jumped them.

Yet how important was that? he must ask himself. He'd come home because of his father's health and would be undercutting everything were he to allow side issues to assume undue importance. They could be sore and suspicious but that was no reason to burden Jordan about the matter.

'All right,' he said finally, sucking skinned knuckles, unaware how tough and hard the quiet 'Rider' appeared in that moment with a smear of blood on his face and dark eyes glinting that way. 'It's forgotten. Go get your horse, Tyran, we're going home.'

'Spoken like a gentleman, Duane,' Leonard gushed as a happy Tyran quit the room. He shook their hands in turn. 'You boys have no idea how important this is to me. You see, a consortium I head up has been negotiating with your father and the Basin Lumber Company to secure some leases in Drumgriff, and these discussions are at a delicate stage. Your dad hates the kid hanging out here, and if he got wind of this shindig tonight—'

'We said there'll be nothing said,' Duane snapped,

heading for the door. 'Do you want it in writing?'

Yet had the brothers' assurances been transcribed, notarised and signed and witnessed by a Justice of the Peace, it still could not have guaranteed against the incident involving the three Everson brothers reaching their father's ears.

It happened the following day when Jordan's attorney-cum-accountant made one of his scheduled visits to Cloud Valley. Turned out the man had been an unseen witness to the whole scene in back of the Domino when the explosion of violence caught him visiting a lady-friend in an adjacent hotel. The man naturally assumed Jordan knew all about it, and by the time he left for Doubletree, that had become the case.

The consequences were predictable. Jesse and Duane were summoned to receive a calling-out for withholding something Jordan claimed a father's right to know. He was caustic but not overly so. Tyran didn't fare so well. The fact that the boy had sneaked out yet again, and had been apparently spying on his brothers and was responsible for them getting involved in a public brawl, was regarded as about the penultimate last straw by his father, who confined him to Cloud Valley for a week.

Yet Jordan saved his real venom for Gray Leonard, and Jesse and Duane were given an insight into the long-running feud between the king of the county and the pretender to his throne in the minutes that followed. It became evident that Leonard had been utilizing every method, both legal and otherwise, to grab a foothold in the Everson empire, most of which, according to the entrepreneur-cum-gambling boss, Jordan had acquired by suspect means.

Sipping watered whiskey, Jordan took the time to

explain why the timber leases of Drumgriff Basin were the prime source of contention.

Leonard alleged that, before lumber was worth a dime in the developing region, Jordan, in order to circumvent tough limitations on monopolies, had formed a combine of citizen-ranchers to apply for and secure leases in the basin, until the Basin Lumber Company had the legal right to log Drumgriff in its entirety. Thereafter he convinced his fellow lessees that they had all made a bad investment and succeeded in buying up their interests for a song. Only then did Jordan reveal he'd secretly signed a huge contract with the Western Railroad Company to supply unlimited lumber for ties, bridges and railroad construction.

'Pretty sneaky, Dad,' Jesse said, yet seemed deeply impressed.

'That's how business is done, mister.' Jordan was unrepentant. He coughed and the ubiquitous Mrs Barker's head appeared round the doorframe. He waved the woman away, coughed again and reached for the whiskey. 'Ever since then that upstart Leonard has been looking to muscle in on the basin, citing illegalities and such rubbish. I suppose I've been softening a little on that front . . .' he paused to slug down a shot, banged the empty glass down hard on the table. 'But not any longer. He's been leading Tyran astray, letting him run up gambling debts and pandering to his weaknesses. But getting him involved in fights with his own brothers is too damned much. The deal on the basin we've been negotiating is dead in the water as of this minute, finished, kaput!'

Duane turned his head as Tyran emitted a choked

sound. The kid looked white as death as he got to his feet.

'For God's sake, don't do that, dad. You just don't understand . . .'

'Don't understand what?' Jordan snapped.

But the boy had no answer.

Seemed nobody knew about the woman until breakfast-time next morning.

The meal had been a mostly silent affair through the ham and eggs, with Duane and Jesse feeling the after-effects of the brawl, and Tyran jittery and pale as he just poked at his food. Beth alone was bright and cheerful, telling them about a fawn she'd seen on the forest edge yesterday, and breaking off occasionally to dart looks at Tyran. The girl had heard all about the incident in Doubletree but it didn't seem to faze her, causing the older brothers to wonder if she might not have learned the trick of deliberately screening out the many unpleasantries in her life and focusing only on the positives. Not such a bad idea on Cloud Valley Ranch in this uncertain springtime of '79, perhaps.

Duane was considering his first cigarette of the day when the tinkle of laughter sounded from the stairs. All heads turned, and moments later Jordan appeared with Clarissa Harte on his arm. He looked ravaged and gaunt but the old defiant glitter was there in his eye as he greeted them genially, then made a small ceremony of seating the woman next to his chair at the head of the table.

When he looked up Duane's chair was empty.

From the deep woods the little family of deer stepped

out to graze the coarse grass of the old ranch. The sun was warm and they drowsed a little as they munched and moved, unaware they had been seen.

Spreading out, they moved slowly up the slope towards the ruins, the young stags, three to four years old, lean and swift and just beginning to feel their power. The does and fawns trailed the antlered males placidly until the breeze changed direction and the scent hit their nostrils, sending them flying for cover which they gained so fast that it was difficult to believe they'd ever been there at all.

Seated on the knoll with his back against the crab-apple tree, Duane grinned and absently fingered his neck and jaw, the former still scarred up some from the shootout here last week, his chin tender and bruised from the ruckus in town.

It was a pretty day in Suspicion Canyon and as the air grew warm the big blue Montanan morning began to smoke faintly.

Montana.

A great place to be this time of year. So why was he thinking of Arizona?

He heard the horse long before he saw it. His sixgun was in his hand by the time the rider appeared from the direction of Little Round Top and Cloud Valley, but he slipped the weapon away well before his brother's searching gaze found him, and he headed in his direction.

'How come I knew I'd find you here, Rider?'

'Not too hard to figure, I guess,' he said, rising. He brushed twigs from his gear as Jesse dismounted. 'What brings you out anyway?'

Jesse let the reins drop carelessly and leaned against the crab-apple tree's gnarled old hide. He appeared tall and invincible as he gazed round at the big blue day. Same old Jesse. And yet, as he'd done before, Duane found himself studying his brother with the certainty that Jesse Everson was a million miles from being a happy man. Something seemed to be missing; he didn't know what it could be.

'You know why,' he replied.

'The old man. Yeah, Jordan's timing always stank as I remember,' Duane responded.

'His timing or his habits never change. He's sick, he's locked himself away on the ranch like a goddamned hermit, some of his family's going to the devil before his eyes and he seems to like only people who kow-tow to him till you want to puke, like that housekeeper. Yet he still plays God, rules the fragging roost and still thinks he's the stud of the West. Suppose you've got to admire that in a way.'

'I don't.'

Jesse's expression was thoughtful as he regarded him.

'You and the old man never did get along, did you?'

'No.'

'Any particular reason?'

Duane folded his arms and studied the northlands haze he remembered from childhood. A haze that glazed the eyes and helped make a wish-dream of anything, everything.

He spoke softly yet with an edge to his voice. 'It was a thousand things but mostly the women. He besmirched Ma's memory with all those tramps, and he's still doing it.'

'So you hate his guts?'

'I didn't say that.'

'Why'd you come back, Duane? I mean, really?'

'Why'd you?'

'Who knows.'

'He thinks we both only came back to make sure we get our share if he dies.'

Jesse shrugged powerful shoulders and turned his face to the sun.

'Sounds just like him. You know, you're right what you just said about him and Ma. She always had more character in her little finger than Jordan's got in his whole crumbling body. And you know something I've never told you, Rider? I hold character more above 'most anything, mainly because I don't have much.' He laughed abruptly. 'By glory, that's some admission to make. Wonder if Ma heard that?'

Both glanced across at the knoll where the headstone stood in dappled sunshine beneath the tree. Memories came crowding in and there was silence for a long slow time, a silence with joy and pain in it, mostly pure joy. Jesse had loved their mother as much as Duane had. They'd bonded as brothers under the mantle of her affection.

'Sure she did,' Duane grunted. Then he frowned. 'Guess she's past fretting over what Jordan does with his life.'

'You know, maybe we're being too tough on the old bastard, man? I mean, it's his house, he's free to live how he likes. Anyway, maybe he's serious about this one. Ty tells me he's been seeing her on and off for quite a spell.' He chuckled at a thought. 'Say, he might marry Blondie then cut us all off without a cent.'

'There's one way to be sure that doesn't happen.'

'What?'

'You stay on when we get him back on his feet. You belong here, Jesse. And he always minded you.'

Jesse instantly changed the subject.

'Let's go to town. We're getting too serious.'

'I've had enough of towns for the time being.'

Jesse's face took on a sly look. 'Maybe we could go find some old pals and gab about the old days?' He gave him a nudge. 'You like all that kind of stuff, I know.' Then realizing Duane still was not responding, he turned serious. 'Then how about us taking a fly at scaring up anybody who might have an angle on just exactly what is going on with our family and the Valley, Bro? You're busting to get to the bottom of things and I guess the same goes for me. Interested?'

Duane deliberated. He certainly was interested, as he knew he should be. But he was still considering when the other spoke again.

'You might bump into Jana. That'd be a bonus, right?'

'What do you mean by that?'

'What do you think I mean? She's gorgeous and you know it. And she still looks at you like she always did, like she never looked at yours truly, by God and by Jesus.'

'Has anyone ever told you you talk too much?'

'Everyone. So, what do you say?'

They rode side by side along a rutted trail, and it was just like the old days with Jesse talking his head off and Duane mostly silent and enjoying it. The long day passed peacefully and pleasantly, the kind of day the county would in time look back upon nostalgically as the calm before the storm.

7

Came the Killers

Monk Hendry sank to his chin in the soapy water, scrubbing at his leathery face and bawling snatches of bawdy songs. Sucking in a deep breath he sank beneath the surface, stayed under until his lungs were ready to burst, then erupted like some breaching sea-creature with a bellowing, bursting roar of exuberance that startled all the horses and not a few of the men.

There were five of each, men and horses. The horses settled for shaking their head-harnesses and stamping uneasily at the commotion, while two of the hard-bitten men muttered in annoyance.

'He's gotta be freezin' in there, damnit,' declared the first. 'So it's a sunny day. But it's a long way from hot, and that water comes from under the ground. Ain't he got feelin's?'

'I know what he has got,' replied the second man, a narrow-faced felon with flat yellow eyes. 'Lungs. Will you just listen to that!'

Monk was singing again, beating the surface of the water with his palms in time. Then he went under, came up with cheeks bulging and sent a plume of water high above his head.

Leckie came across from the horses with a plug of chaw tobacco in his jaw and a half-grin on his hawk face.

'You plan on gettin' out of that thing today or tomorrow?' he wanted to know.

But the bather submerged again and his skinny white shanks shot up in the air. Then his head reappeared wearing a cowl of soap froth that gave him the appearance of an evil, bearded gnome.

'You know how long since I had a hot tub, Sunny Jim?' he barked.

Stub Leckie knew, to the day. Seven weeks ago when the bunch had dared stop over at a whistle-stop tank-town on the Western Railroad, which boasted no hot tub but did feature a ten-thousand-gallon tank in which Monk had swum long and exuberantly until hypothermia overtook him and he'd had to be dragged out and heated up by the fire.

The outlaw loved to bathe. And with good reason. He looked bad, smelt bad, was bad. Washing at least took care of the smell for a while. There was nothing he could do, or wanted to do, about either his looks or character.

'All right, fetch a man a towel,' he decided, then vanished yet again, arms and legs flailing furiously as though he were freestyling down the indoor pool at the Olympic Club in Kansas City, not lolling about in a rusted horse-trough on a desolate stretch of plains country known as the Sioux Strip beneath a clanking old wind-pump which had rattled and rusted unattended out here for ten years ever since the railroad didn't come.

The visionary who'd installed the Cameron pump and erected the plank-and-batten 'hotel' which had long since been blown away by the endless plains winds, had taken out a map, estimated where the railroad would go through, calculated the logical trail for the cattle herds driving north to south to take, figured the exact spot where they would intersect, went to work, then sat down and waited for opportunity and wealth to come rushing him. He was still waiting hopefully in some flophouse in Denver while the odd trapper, drifter or badman taking advantage of his trough from time to time might ponder idly just what sort of fool he was indebted to for this little luxury in the heart of noplace.

The 'towel' Leckie brought back was actually a blue army-blanket taken from the body of a man they'd murdered in the Dakotas. 'Chowtime!' he bellowed and they got busy as Monk hopped and hollered about as naked as a jaybird and ugly as mortal sin beneath this innocent sun.

Monk Hendry would be fifty next birthday if the rangers, marshals and bounty hunters didn't overtake him beforehand. Stoop-shouldered and pot-bellied with a hide as soft and white as a mud lizard's underbelly, he moved with a quick, pigeon-toed walk, swinging long ape-like arms. His head was small with a fringe of ginger hair framing his spotty bald dome. A ragged moustache hid his bulging mouth and the slate-coloured eyes were red-rimmed and watery.

They couldn't have nicknamed him anything but Monk, as in monkey. Yet he wore the name with pride. For unimpressive though he certainly was, he was a born leader of men and a natural killer whose notoriety had finally caught up with him. He no longer dared visit cities or even the towns any more. With his likeness plastered across the West, he was condemned to exist, like an animal, in the wild and lonesome reaches of the deserts, mountains, or here on Sioux Strip. He lived on what he could steal and was always available for hire to those who might be able to track him down through the secret outlaw network.

Business was slack at the moment and his hench-men were chafing at the inactivity and rebelling against their spartan surroundings. Not Monk. Rich or poor, relaxed and safe or running like a dog, he lived for the moment and never fretted about tomor-row. He'd had more hard times than hot suppers but somehow things always took a turn for the better for him eventually. All he had to do was wait and enjoy himself as he went along.

The food his woman prepared was plain but fill-ing. The killer ate ravenously and never stopped talk-ing. He hopped up and about to get salt and ketchup, cursed his horse for the mean eye it was putting on him, counselled Trey Connor against the evils of cohabiting with Indian women and did his level best, around a jawful of grits and pone bread, to remember and render all the verses of 'Bringing In The Sheafs'.

The sound of the shot sounded flat and faint in the distance. As one, the four men and the slender woman in faded denim pants jumped to stare south where tiny dots of movement were barely visible against the tan and green of the plain.

'Most likely Amos,' speculated Flowers. 'He's due.'

'What if it ain't?' queried Connor.

'What sort of question is that, boy?' growled Monk. He rolled his slate eyes at the others. 'Is that a dumb question or ain't it?'

Heads nodded. It was dumb. Monk had chosen their campsite deliberately. A tin trough and a Cameron wind-pump surrounded by wide open miles of nothing represented a guarantee that nothing that walked, breathed or carried a Colt .45 could get within miles of them without being sighted. Whoever it was coming across the flat country – and they could see now it was two men on horseback – would either be familiar or be dead.

It was half an hour of coffee and hardtack biscuits later before Leckie used his battered old field-glasses to identify Casper Amos positively. The gang's scout trailsman was yet to have his likeness appear on any Wanted dodgers, so he was the one they sent to towns for supplies, information, to scout out potential targets and maintain contact with the owlhoot underground.

The closer the riders drew the brighter Monk's mood.

'It's gotta be a client,' he insisted, shading his eyes with his hand. He squinted hard, then nodded. 'Well-dressed joker on a flash-lookin' horse. Gotta be a daddy big bucks lookin' for someone ugly to take care of his fat wife so he can set up light house-keepin' with a bad tempered waitress less than half his age, heh, heh.'

'What if he ain't, Monk?' asked Connor, who resembled a stable door in coveralls. 'Can I claim that hoss?'

Monk just chuckled deep as his liver. He was sure

he was reading the well-dressed stranger's brand right, so sure indeed that he swaggered out to meet them with a big agreeable grin, yet his fist was wrapped round the silky oak stock of his sixshooter, just in case.

He didn't need the gun. Casper Amos yelled a cheery greeting, then introduced the man in the silk shirt astride the appaloosa as 'the client from Doubletree'.

Monk welcomed the stranger like a brother.

'Hey, Rider,' grinned the ramrod as the cook clanged his triangle for supper. 'You too good to chow down with us workin' stiffs now?'

Duane returned the grin. 'Sorry, have to eat at the house these nights, Lee. I'll explain later.'

'Between you and me, I wouldn't risk this man's cookin' if I had a choice,' the man cracked, then ducked the cook's swipe behind an upraised hand before disappearing into the cookhouse where the hands were already sitting down to eat.

For a moment Duane felt a twinge of envy. Simple food and easy company with no tantrums, secrets, sidelong glances or weighty silences here. He sighed and headed for the house. He felt he had no option these days. The dust had settled since the incident in town the previous week but the atmosphere remained uncertain. Tyran was quiet, most likely still sulking. Beth was agreeable in her determinedly cheerful way, while Jesse, of course, was the life of the party and provided the necessary oil to help keep this creaky clan machinery working after a fashion.

And Jordan had not offended since his breakfast-with-a-blonde morning, although it would be foolish to imagine he might regret that episode. Yet he did seem in brighter spirits even though the worrying illness continued to keep him confined to the house; there was a whisper that he had plans for a visit to town, for what purpose Duane didn't know.

He was about to find out.

He hadn't noticed the brougham and pair drawn up by the house gates until now. He stopped and stared, for visitors were rare and growing rarer at the Valley these days, with the odd blonde exception. Crossing to the rig he found the driver dozing in his seat, and awoke him by rapping on the splashboard.

'Doc?' the man sputtered. Then he frowned. 'Oh, Mr Duane, I believe?'

'Right. You called me Doc. Is this Doc Greenlease's rig by any chance?'

Indeed it was, so he discovered. According to the man, Doc had been persuaded to accompany his sometime assistant out to Cloud Valley in the hope Mr Everson might relent and allow him to run the stethoscope over him after she furnished him the information he was waiting on.

Duane felt himself grinning as he strode for the house. Jana here? This augured well for a brighter evening. He had no notion what brought her out. But he was happy she'd inveigled Doc into accompanying her, even if it did cause fireworks.

He found them waiting supper for him. The atmosphere was cool but not frosty, with Doc at the opposite end of the long table from his father, and Jana welcoming him with a smile from her chair between the twins. Jesse greeted him with a wave and informed him in a half-joking way that Jordan had refused Greenlease's offer to examine him, but at least the 'two old mossyhorns' were talking again.

The meal was not long under way before he learned the reason for the visit. Seemed there was an important anniversary coming up and Jordan, a sometime churchgoer before his illness, was insisting he attend church the following Sunday. He'd submitted a written request for a special service to the preacher who'd taken advantage of Greenlease's and Jana's visit to a patient down the trail to send out his reply to the effect that the church was available for an early private service Sunday next at seven a.m.

'What's the occasion?' Duane asked his father.

'It's Saint Gabriel's day and just happens to be your mother's and my wedding anniversary,' came the reply. 'Twenty-nine years next Sunday.' He raised his wine-glass. 'To a fine lady, Simone Everson.'

Jesse's and Duane's eyes met across the silver, crystal and overflowing bowls of flowers. Surprised and pleased by this turn of events, they raised the goblets to each other, then to Jana, the bringer of the good word. Her smile in response seemed a little rueful. Duane understood how anxious she was to have Doc back to treating Jordan, but it seemed that was still some time ahead.

The housekeeper and two maids brought in the next course, the girls serving, Mrs Barker supervising. She sniffed at Doc who glowered back; no love lost there. Jordan appeared mildly amused by their reactions; it was quite possible that he enjoyed seeing the visible tension between two people at loggerheads over who should have the distinction of treating him.

Jordan did not look well tonight, rarely did these days. Jana, by contrast, was stunning in a vivid dress

that would have looked too flamboyant on most
women, and seemed totally at home at this intimi-
dating table as she ate with gusto, drank generously
and managed to keep the conversation going whenever it flagged.

An unexpected thought ambushed the quiet man
from the South when he found himself musing; this
girl would make some lucky stiff a great little wife.
Then found himself studying Jesse closely as he
leaned across the table to chink glasses with Jana in
some toast he didn't catch. They would be perfect
together. Both were handsome, outgoing, sure of
themselves and popular with just about everybody.
And momentarily he envied people with those quali-
ties even if he would not change his sometimes solitary yet totally satisfying way of living for any reason
under the sun.

It was late when the visitors left. Jesse and Duane
insisted on riding escort back to Doubletree, not
getting back until two with a huge white moon riding
the sky and wolves singing from the escarpment.

They found the headquarters asleep but for the
rugged-up men with guns patrolling the perimeters;
their father's light burning dimly in the den.

For a moment it almost felt as it had when they
were kids and 'home' had simply meant that. Home.
But the feeling couldn't last, for a man couldn't go
back.

Sunday dawned bitter and bleak with a mean wind
blowing birds across the sky like scattered pieces of
paper. There was the threat of rain in the air and the
driver and gun-guard shivered atop the high seat of
the enclosed four-wheel coach-and-four as it carried

the Cloud Valley party down Placer Street then swung wide to make the left into Border and headed for the church.

Duane and Jesse waited for their father by their horses at the hitch rail in front of high-steepled St Gabriel's. They were double-checking the security and finding all as it should be.

Two Valley bodyguards were in place at the boarded-up barn directly opposite, and the brothers themselves would stand watch in the vestibule throughout the ceremony. This was considered by all as ample security in Doubletree, and Jesse was making cracks about how lucky they'd been to draw the indoors detail in light of the return to almost winter conditions.

Jordan would not even turn up to a witch-burning without a lady on his arm, but at least he had displayed some discretion and a sense of occasion today by stepping down with a respectable matron and old family friend to beat their way into the church against the yammering wind. Tyran and Beth followed and all vanished inside where a small group of friends and others who'd been close to Simone were already assembled.

Duane and Jesse mounted the steps, where they paused to make a final survey. Border Street was slowly disappearing behind a needlepointed squall of ice-drops which beat a tattoo against the isinglass windows of the heavy coach as the driver manoeuvred it round to the lee side of the building. The muffled-up shotgun-guard joined them and the three hurried inside and shut the doors firmly behind them.

It was some time later before the organ began to

wheeze and groan, and as though it was a signal, a rig of some description appeared out of Placer, hesitated a moment then turned and headed uncertainly towards St Gabriel's.

'I swear you couldn't find your way to hell even if it was signposted and you had a map tattooed on your elbow, Milton Briggs!' the hunched-up woman in the heavy blanket-coat complained as the single horse in the shafts of the curricle designed for two plodded miserably past Rafferty's Music Emporium and the drygoods store. 'They said the first left, this is the second.'

'Will you hush up and let a man concentrate, woman.' The driver might have been twenty or sixty, there was no telling the way he was bundled up with the collar of an old Confederate greatcoat turned up beneath his low-brimmed hat, beady eyes squinting out over a striped muffler.

The driver appeared to be looking straight ahead searching for landmarks, whereas in reality his focus was on the old barn with its side door banging in the wind and looking as if it could blow over if that bitch wind should pick up another five or six miles an hour.

Jordan Everson's gun-guards were barely visible. But the hawk-eyes of Monk Hendry ferreted them out easily enough, mainly because he knew exactly where to look. He also knew that right about this minute the son of a Coloradan cow-thief and a one-eyed gun-tipper wearing a tall black hat tied on with a leather string were making their stealthy way through that abandoned building towards the front with clubs in hand. Leastwise they'd better be.

The Valley guards had sighted them, were leaning

forward fingering the rifles in gloved hands.

'Couldn't navigate a plate of beans through a cow's digestive tract, neither you could!' Monk bawled at his companion. The wind snatched his words away but the men at the barn clearly heard the woman's response:

'You might be right, you bum, but I'd sure recognize the result. It'd look perzackly like you!'

The sentries grinned and were moving back out of reach of the wind when there was a sickening thud and the one in the window slumped unconscious across the unpainted sill, dropping his heavy rifle with a great clatter. His companion at the doorway cursed and whirled with his weapon sweeping up, but too late. The hickory club came against the side of his head with a bang and he tumbled out of sight as Monk and his woman sprang from the rickety curricle with sixshooters in their fists.

Monk's simian features were alive with excitement as he hissed 'Yes!' only waiting until his two henchmen, who'd done their work so well, came running into sight from behind the building before spinning and charging across open space for the church.

The horses tied up at the long rail were startled by the sudden flurry of movement and jerked back against their ties. But it was the black mustang, which Rider Duane claimed to be 'the best watchdog in Arizona', that reared high, emitting a shrill whistle as the four running figures rushed past making for the heavy oaken doors with the iron hinges and worn brass handles.

Which slowly began to open!

Monk faltered in his stride with a choked-off curse. This wasn't supposed to happen! Then that fool horse sounded again and the tall doors closed with a bang seconds before the woman reached them.

Inside, an alarmed Duane was already legging it for the belfry stairs as Jesse dropped the cross-bar into place to hold the doors fast as shoulders thudded ineffectually against them.

'Get down!' Duane bawled at the top of his lungs as the worshippers turned in alarm. 'Jesse, get them down before—'

His voice broke off as a side door jolted open and a figure as anonymous and menacing as the men he'd just glimpsed in the street came barrelling through with a revolver in either hand, shouting: 'Pay-back time, Everson!' as he jerked triggers to fill the confined space with insane sound, gunbarrels blossoming like flowers of death.

Duane's desperate glance saw Jordan smother the woman protectively with his body as three pews of people and the preacher attempted to get down under cover. Duane's gun was still coming up when Jesse's .45 opened up directly below to add painfully to the gun thunder now rocking the nave. His shooting was wild yet it sent the gunman diving for an archway off to his right where he disappeared, his wild cry rising above the head-jarring reverberations of the Colts;

'Monk, where the hell are you?'

'Jesse!' Duane hollered. But the tall figure was already racing down the aisle with a smoking gun to head for the archway, leaving Duane a vital moment to gain the belfry landing and the window there.

He looked out. The street was empty. But the wild-eyed horses were all staring towards the east corner, indicating that the others had to be making for the east door which the first gunman had entered by.

It was a fifteen-foot leap to the floor. Duane landed hard, lurched, caroomed off the stone baptismal font then vaulted the waist-high organ to hit the carpet running, frantically trying to reach the open doorway before they did.

'Watch out, boy!'

His father's voice. Duane hurled himself full length, Colt sprouting from his upraised arm as the heavy man with the shotgun came surging through the door, stained yellow slicker flapping wildly as his eyes hunted for a target.

Duane triggered.

Instantly the shotgunner was flung staggering back against the door with white-hot death impaling him. Reflexes twitched and his shotgun discharged shatteringly into the ceiling to bring plaster and woodwork raining down upon him as his body slumped against the door, his face wreathed in gunsmoke.

Duane was up.

Somebody was crashing against the door trying to open it inwards but the body was blocking it. He emptied his pistol through the six-inch chink between door and frame in a continuous rolling roar. A man howled in agony and another voice was heard to cry: 'Horses, goddamnit! We're gettin' out of here!'

Fifty feet away in the baptistery, Jesse heard that cry and was heartened by it. Yet cold sweat was streaking down his face as he forced himself across the room towards the door of a smaller utility room in back. The gunman had to be behind that door; it was the only place he could be.

He covered three paces when he heard a faint rustling sound. He triggered instantly and drilled a hole in the flimsy door. Retaliatory fire exploded from behind the door which suddenly erupted with splintering bullet holes and hot lead flew wildly through the baptistery. Jesse ducked low with a sharp burning sensation along his left forearm. From the floor he triggered back, the snarl of his .45 suddenly engulfed by the bellow of a 12 gauge directly behind him. The door all but disintegrated under the impact, and he saw Duane standing there with the dead man's smoking weapon angled at the floor.

It was suddenly painfully quiet in the church of St Gabriel as what remained of the door sagged slowly open. The brothers stared. The man lay twisted on the floor. They didn't need to look twice to know he was dead. It was only as their hearing began to recover that they realized the distant thudding sounds they could hear were those of fading hoof-beats.

Their first thought was for their father. But they found him unscathed, cursing and hollering for the sheriff. It was the preacher who'd been killed, struck by the bullet intended for Everson when he'd thrown himself upon the woman and borne her to the floor. A mother of three had been struck in the shoulder, was moaning softly in the arms of her husband. The whole affair had only occupied a brief snatch of time, yet the place looked like a battleground with terrified people sprawled everywhere beneath a pall of gunsmoke.

Well before Buck Tune arrived leading a crowd of ashen-faced towners, the slowly recovering survivors at St Gabriel's were agreed upon one thing. The killers had come gunning for Jordan Everson. Just as he'd long feared they would.

8

Wolves in the Woods

The posse raced on through the foothills following the killers' clear tracks along all the crooks and turns of the canyon trail. They travelled at a laboured run, for the gradient had been steepening steadily ever since the sign led them up off the plains at Simpson's Crossing. Here the bed of the watercourse was so rough and jumbled with boulders the tracks disappeared completely from time to time. But every hundred yards or so, Duane, riding beside a grim-jawed Sheriff Tune behind the tall figure of Jesse, caught the occasional glimpse of a spatter of dried blood upon a rock or patch of grass.

Jesse was maintaining a pace faster than some felt wise, and some of the mounts were already tiring badly. But the theory of Jesse, who just naturally had seemed to assume the role of posse boss, was that with one of their number wounded, this could easily slow the gang eventually, even force them to halt.

Duane glanced back as they emerged onto an

open slope. He was just in time to see the two lagging possemen abruptly swing their horses and head back the way they'd come. His jaws tightened. The blacksmith and postmaster had had enough without clocking up even one full day in the saddle.

They were not the first defectors. Fifteen grim-faced men had stormed out of town that morning, all primed on righteous wrath and ready to ride as far as it took. Their passion hadn't lasted. This latest defection cut their strength to under ten. Gazing up at the slopes and crags crouching beneath a stormy sky, where the killers had gone, he sensed even more strongly that they were in for a long hard haul. He'd not expected their quarry to make for the mountains, and worried that they might plan to strike clear across Chain Range to the Divide, taking their chances with snow, ice and even spring blizzards, rather than face the wrath of the men of Doubletree. But exactly how many men might still be riding with the brothers and the lawman if the hunt went on too long was now something he wouldn't try to guess.

Tall in the saddle and sucking on a black cigar, Jesse led them over a humpbacked hill into a tight little valley encircled by walls of red sandstone. Their sudden appearance startled a bunch of wild cattle gathered at a pool to drink. They scattered with loud sniffs, tossing widespread horns, the calves fleeing after them holding their tails curled above their backs.

Duane shot a look at the lowering skies. If it rained heavily the sign could be washed away. He hit the horse with heels and it picked up its pace to draw abreast of his brother's long-legged chestnut. He was about to speak as they went sweeping around a stand of blue cedars, when abruptly a flock of buzzards rose noisily from behind a fallen tree and rose into the windy sky, cawing and croaking in anger at being disturbed.

The man was dead, shot through the head.

He lay on his back in the grass, and the birds had been busy.

'The one we winged in the doorway,' Jesse breathed as Duane slid to ground. 'But how'd he ride this far with half his head blown off?'

'He didn't.' Duane stood lean and hard-faced at the dead man's feet as the horsemen encircled them. He pointed. 'The blood on his leg's long dried where that bullet busted the bone. You can see it sticking through. But the head wound's fresh, maybe just an hour or two old. . . .'

'So what the hell happened?' a red-faced posse-man wanted to know. 'Who shot him?'

'His buddies,' Duane replied stonily, gazing up at the sheriff. 'Who else?'

'What do you make of it, Duane?' said Buck Tune.

'Seems pretty plain to me,' he replied, returning slowly to Joker. He fitted boot to stirrup but paused to stare back at the grisly spectacle. 'I reckon that fellow rode as far as he could with that leg. When he couldn't go on they killed him.'

'But why, man?' Jesse puzzled.

Duane settled into his saddle. 'My guess is they knew we'd catch him and that he might talk too much. So they made sure he didn't say anything.'

He let that sink in as a gusty wind came surging through the trees and the first spots of cold rain hit. The grave faces of store clerks, cowboys, saloon loafers and a portly undertaker now all too clearly registered understanding of exactly what breed of man they were so eager to overtake. Yet shockingly, it appeared to Duane that the man worst affected was his brother. Jesse continued to stare at the dead man with his face the colour of old pipeclay.

Uncertainty and apprehension rippled through the ranks until Tune slapped his horse with his quirt and barked, "All right, let's get on with it!'

They had covered less than a mile in worsening light when the skies opened up and the rain came down like the Biblical flood.

Monk knew his famous luck was smiling on him again after the débâcle in Doubletree when they reached the shelter of this huge rocky overhang just as the deluge began. He hopped and skipped about the horses in flapping mackinaw and sodden hat, then threw ape arms wide and bawled, 'Hallelujah! Told you Lady Luck always looks after your boy. Four hundred fraggin' bloodhounds wouldn't be able to pick up our sign by the time this little freshet is through.'

His enthusiasm often proved the infectious glue that held them together but it didn't seem to be working now. Still in their saddles, the man and the woman – just three survivors out of six – stared blankly down at this grinning grimacing gnome, then glanced backtrail.

Maybe in retrospect now they could see the risk in leaving the wounded Leckie behind for that hick posse to find and interrogate. But did he have to be gunned down like a dog? The man and woman weren't mourning, just wondering if he'd turn on them one day as he had with Stub Leckie.

'Hey!' Monk barked, turning mean. 'I know what you're thinkin'. Trouble is you don't understand. Stub was the only one who knew where we're headin'.' He spread bony knuckled hands. 'My special hideaway. Iffen I'd left him alive that tin-star and his dingle-dodie towners could've beat us up there. You'd rather that, mebbe?'

'I knew you'd have good reason, Sugar,' gaunt Zara said. She frowned. 'So where are we going anyway?'

'You can't guess?' Monk said with a cunning smirk. 'That's pretty abysmal.'

He pronounced it 'abissmal'. Flowers scowled from his saddle.

'You mean abysmal,' he said, using the correct pronunciation.

Monk's face split into his trademark grin. 'I mean abissmal, pretty boy. Like in abyss. The Abyss.'

Chinook turned away from the hungry possemen who were making pretty free with his canned supplies.

'So, they finally got round to trying it, huh?'

'What?' Duane asked, fingers fashioning a quirley.

'I'm talkin' about all them who wanted your daddy dead, of course, boy.'

'Are you saying you expected this?' Duane was terse. It was the following day. The rain had swept away towards the Dakotas overnight ahead of a day of mocking mountain sunshine which spilled warmly now over a mountainscape washed clean of all tracks other than those cut deep by the iron-shod wheels of the lumbering timber-jinkers in the distance across the basin.

The snap decision to make the punishing climb to visit the mountain man had been his alone. Even Jesse and Tune had argued he was grabbing at straws. But he'd stood fast. Without one lead or piece of sign to bless himself with following the deluge, he'd come to see the only man in the mountains who just might come up with some notion, idea, theory or wild guess that might help.

He didn't care who disagreed. Nor was he interested in listening to off-handed remarks about his father. The usually quiet and controlled Rider Duane looked hard-edged and flinty as he stared back at him with an unlit cigarette jutting from the corner of his mouth. Tough. Tougher than Chinook had ever seen him.

The mountain man nodded as though in understanding. He put a match to the bowl of his feathered Sioux pipe, then held out the vesta to the tip of Duane's cigarette. Both men drew deeply. Chinook flicked a thoughtful glance across at Jesse who stood alone by the muddied horses. Finally he nodded his wise old head.

'Your daddy was just too big, too successful, too tough, and got mixed up with too many women not to make a power of enemies, young Rider,' he felt he had to remark. 'But he ain't a bad man and never was, and I hope you get those that tried to do him in. Now, what can I do for you? Before they clean me out of house and home, that is.'

Duane was mollified. He hunkered down and commenced sketching in the dirt with a stick.

'You know these mountains better than any he-coon or grizzly, old-timer. Now this is where we lost their sign, at Moosehead Point. I'm at a loss to even guess where in tarnation they were heading, though judging by the headlong way they travelled, they were sure heading someplace, not just running blind. But where? Whitewater Plateau maybe? Or do you reckon they could be thinking of tackling the Divide?'

'Hmm, odd route to take, cutting up towards Black Tree Fork thataway. . . .' Chinook rubbed his chin and the faded blue eyes were sharp on Duane's face. He was totally absorbed by the problem now. 'Real pros, you reckon they are?'

'Had to be, the way they went about their work.' Duane shook his dark head. 'And the way they finished that wounded man off. . . . Yeah, I'd say they are professionals OK. Gun scum. But not stupid. They're not just running, they're running some-where. I'm sure of it.'

'Well, that makes it mighty interestin' on account of, if I'm figurin' out where they could be headin' right, it'd make good sense for killers on the run. It's a place to hell and gone up nigh the timberline and further north even than the bear hunters ever get to go. Wilderness, boy, real honest to God mountain wilderness so big you could miss findin' a Kansas City bordello with all its lights burnin' iffen you didn't know exactly where to look. It's hid, it's remote and the way it's laid out by mother nature it's like a natural fortress where a few tolerable tough roosters could hold out against an army if they wanted. Matter of fact, that's perzackly what happened years ago in the Injun Wars. Sound like the sort of lay-out these hardcases of yours might know about?'

'Just could be,' Duane replied with mounting

eagerness. 'Do I know this place?'

'Nope, guess not. Just me and a bunch of Teton Sioux and Blackfeet, and the odd outlaw on the run would about cover those who do. The Sioux are them that showed it to me.' The old man winked conspiratorially. 'I believe I'd know it better than 'most any white man, even this killer of yours. Interested?

'Sounds the best hope I've got, mainly because I don't have any others.'

Chinook sat on his three-legged camp-stool, jammed the stem of his long curved pipe between his teeth, locked his hands around an updrawn knee and leaned back comfortably.

After a pause he began to talk and draw on the ground.

A dark wind blew down from Monarch Mountain, and small live things in the brush scurried for cover in frantic haste, not knowing what had frightened them. A cold old moon bathed canyon, cliff and upland meadow in its pallid light while men spoke in hushed tones of mystery, death and hidden dangers, and ghouls and undertakers rubbed dry hands in eager expectation of when the guns would begin to roar and the blood to flow.

For the lawless had slipped their leashes in Bear Lake County and these springtime weeks in the wild mountains were truly the seasons of the gun.

Duane crouched motionless as an Indian on the fringe of a hackberry thicket on a lofty ledge overlooking the Abyss. He'd been staring down for a long spell into the vast and primitive chasm gouged by careless nature out of a mountainside, which today appeared to be dreaming a little under a feeble high country sun, for so long that his eyes were red-rimmed and gritty with strain.

Almost completely concealed in the thicket behind, Joker stood motionless but for his eyes, which, like the man's, continued to play over the contorted landscape below. It was as though the animal knew exactly what was going on, and Duane would swear he did.

This was high up, far higher than anyone would expect any fugitive to run. In the wake of the deluge, trying to second-guess the killers, Duane's best guess had been that they might cut north-east along the old Catamount Mine trail then make a run for the Canadian border. But if Chinook's assessment proved correct, they would have had to cut almost due west from the murder site north-east of Drumgriff Basin to tackle the brutal climb over Skyline Saddle, ford Roaring River west of Hacksaw Cliff then lash horses and pack mules up and over the steeply climbing five-mile hump of Saddleback and then follow the ridgelines up several thousand feet to reach their destination.

He still had no proof they'd headed for this geological nightmare land, was relying entirely upon the mountain man's speculation and the brown-paper maps and sketches he had in his pocket. The deeply sunken basin was ten miles wide in places and gouged its way darkly and deeply in under the very shadows of the Divide at its western perimeter where the volcano slept.

It made horse sense that the gang would never have undertaken such a brutal journey as this and not have the sanctuary of the Abyss as their goal. And he had to admit it appeared a perfect hideaway.

He knuckled his strained eyes and resumed his vigil.

It was the third day of the hunt. The cracks in the posse ranks which had begun to appear the first day had by now expanded into gulches and ravines. The storekeeper-mayor had retired the previous day, suffering saddle sores and exhaustion and taking his two clerks with him. The defections had continued apace and now even the sheriff was talking of turning back.

Maybe Duane could understand Tune's explanation that he'd never expected their quarry to run so far so fast, and that he could not in conscience leave his town without law any longer than it would now take him and his deputies to get back from this point. Yet he still resented it. This was no bunch of petty thieves or chicken-rustlers they were hunting here, as he kept reminding them. They were responding to a murder operation carried out by professional killers. Would Buck Tune ever head up a more desperately important manhunt? Not goddamn likely.

The horse clicked his jaws. He was staring fixedly down over the thrusting rimrock.

Sharply, Duane swung about to peer down again. At first he saw nothing but the pinnacles and spires of wind-tortured stone and the caverned cliff-faces rearing up like the battlement walls of giants' castles which surrounded and fortified the entire basin. To the west, the long-extinct volcano known as Thunder Mountain reared a thousand feet into the sky, fearsome no longer. Not even the Ancient Ones of the Tribes knew how long it was since the last cataclysmic time the mountain had ripped itself apart to send a million tons of lava spewing down into the Abyss, leaving behind great frozen black rivers of stone forming eternal tiger-stripes against the ochre stone of the basin's floor.

It was against one of these broad black traces that first the horse and now the man caught the faintest stir of movement.

It was down in the north-eastern corner where the faintly discernible snake of the narrow entrance pass, the Slot, was visible, exactly where Chinook had said it would be. And there they were, some five hundred feet lower than his position and a good mile distant, a trio of antlike riders and packhorses fording a sparkling mountain stream, then crossing an open sandy space before vanishing into teetering rock pinnacles and cliff shadows.

Duane knew he was catching his first glimpse of his quarry since seeing them go storming off through the streets of Doubletree with one of their number swaying drunkenly in his saddle.

Only now did he risk raising his field-glasses. For a while he focused on the talus-littered cavern sector where the riders had vanished. But then he turned his attention westward, and let the instrument play slowly and carefully until he found what he was looking for: a stream gushing from the base of a yellow rock wall directly beneath a solitary miserable-looking pine clinging to the rimrock above.

Chinook's sketches were all dead accurate, just as he'd known they must be.

He blinked at the sight.

Ten minutes later he rode in to interrupt the liveryman's address to his fellow manhunters. The man dropped his eyes guiltily as Duane swung down, while others averted their gaze. Only the sheriff and

Jesse met his querying look. It was Jesse who spoke.

'Seems we've got a rebellion on our hands, man. Ezekiel's had enough and Buck here is ready to take them back.' He turned his head and spat. 'Catch the whiff of blue funk, or is that just my imagination?'

'Now see here, Jesse Everson!' the sheriff protested, but Duane cut him off.

'It's all right, Sheriff. We could wrangle all day, maybe even shame some of you into staying. But the fact is the people we're chasing are down there in the Abyss where it's going to be ten times more danger-ous than anything we've seen before. There's no telling how long it could take to make contact, and when we do . . .'

Here he paused deliberately, then said quite distinctly, 'When we do, we don't want to find ourselves relying on any man who might go to water just when you can't afford to have him do that.' He gestured with an air of finality. 'Me and Jesse will go on, maybe Younger Bear too?' He glanced at Chinook's impassive Sioux scout, whom he'd insisted they take with them. The man nodded firmly. He went o:. 'When you get back tell our folks we're all fine and that we won't be taking any fool risks.'

'Well said, *amigo*,' Jesse said, taking him by the arm and leading him out of earshot. Then, astonishingly, his confident manner evaporated before Duane's eyes. 'Rider, are we sure about this? I mean, just the three of us going in after a whole bunch of them down into that goddamned pit in hell? Chinook says a handful of Blackfeet held out down there against a hundred Sioux, remember?'

'Are you saying we should quit?' Duane demanded.

'Well, we've given this one hell of a try, man. But with everybody else heading home we could easy find ourselves outnumbered, outsmarted and killed. These bastards are pros, even you said that.'

Duane studied his brother's face. It was like seeing a stranger. For a moment he was shaken, seeing not only his plans for the next desperate hours looking suddenly uncertain, but maybe his entire future. He'd been relying on his brother in both respects. Now he was no longer sure.

But in an instant he was calm.

'We're going in,' he said evenly. 'You, me, and Younger Bear. We have to.'

'Whatever you say.'

They left a short time later with Jesse leading the way followed by the Sioux trailsman and Duane bringing up the rear. They didn't look back at the shamefaced straggle of citizens grouped around the camp-fire. Each of the trio was focused on what lay ahead, and both brothers were checking out their guns as the timber swallowed them. The scout looked at the sky as though praying to his gods that he might survive this eerie place known to the Sioux Old Ones as the Tomb In The Sky.

'Tomb In The Sky?' The woman stared into the pot on the small fire, then looked up. 'What sort of name is that to give a place anyway?'

'It's the best name in the world on account it's the name of the place that's gonna save our fine pink hides, Zara baby.'

Monk Hendry's meagre fringe of dusty-pink hair was flapping round his jug ears in the knifing wind that came whistling through the jagged stone spires and boomed around the caverns. Of the group he appeared least affected by their punishing climb to one of the least hospitable landscapes on the entire mountain chain which wound its imperious way from the Canadian border down to New Mexico.

He was freezing but refused to shiver.

He was still seething over the near disaster at Doubletree, yet gave no sign.

He meant to survive no matter what.

'Well, I have to say it's as good as you promised,' observed the other man. 'Only one track in and we've got it covered from here.' He took out a beautiful silver-plated pistol and rolled it along the sleeve of his black leather quarter-coat. 'If that posse from Hicksville follows us this far then we can pick them off like quail.'

Times like this, Monk Hendry was doubly glad he'd kept feeding those large amounts of hard cash which he could ill afford to this man in order to keep him with the bunch. Times like this, a man really needed a genuine sixgunner *segundo* like Ringo Flowers by his side.

He grinned. Flowers' name always amused him. Such a name for such a man. Doubtless his parents had given their son a manly handle like 'Ringo' to offset the delicacy of his surname. But Monk believed that had he been christened Periwinkle Flowers he would still be about the most dangerous man in Montana Territory.

Then his expression soured.

Too bad Flowers had not lived up to his rep down at Doubletree and put Everson in the ground, hitches and hick heroics notwithstanding.

And digging into a deep pocket of his badly

stained weather coat for his chaw, he shook his head and kicked a bit of wood towards the fire. It should have worked like clockwork! The planning was right, the timing impeccable, the time, weather and venue ideal for a good quick killing. And it would have gone right but for those two men unexpectedly posted inside the church doors who'd sprung the rhythm and timing of the whole operation to such an extent that in the end they'd been lucky to get away with just two pards dead and Leckie nursing a wounded wing.

Cursing, Monk got behind a basalt boulder out of the wind, cut himself a generous plug of tobacco and thrust it into one cheek. Chewing powerfully, he squinted round at the twisted and tortured landscape with its frozen rivers of black lava which looked as if they'd ceased flowing just yesterday instead of thousands of years ago. Like Flowers said, perfect. He felt grateful to Stub Leckie for telling him about this hideaway. Poor old Stub.

His woman had now clambered up into the cave above, where she was keeping watch on the single, steep-walled pass trail into the Abyss close by through field-glasses. Out on the wide stone apron, Flowers overhauled his twin guns with total concentration.

He nodded grimly. Right now, he almost hoped they would come. He was ready.

9

The Devil's Abyss

The pebble he dropped struck rock and clattered away to silence at the bottom of the pit at Duane's feet. Then it was silent again but for the murmur of the waters flowing freely across the littered base of the deep stone hole forty feet below. This was a subterranean creek which, according to Chinook and Younger Bear, only appeared briefly at this point at the end of a mile-long journey underground from somewhere beyond the volcano before angling downwards on its underground journey for an indeterminate distance, finally discharging into the Abyss to form one of its principal rock streams.

Duane glanced back upwards. Jesse appeared strained, the Sioux a little awed. He didn't blame either man, for what this place was, and the use to which he intended putting it, must alarm the former and arouse deep superstitions in the latter.

'What'd Chinook say the Sioux called this place, *amigo*?' he asked, his voice echoing a little down here on his ledge some thirty feet below ground level where the two were standing.

'Death Song Cave,' came the response. Younger Bear gestured. 'In the old battle when the Sioux laid siege to the Blackfeet who were forted in the Abyss, the wounded warriors would come to this place in their fine robes to sing the Death Song until they fell. Their bodies lay below until they were just broken white bones and the stream carried them away down into the Abyss to be scattered by the waters and the winds.'

Duane nodded. This story tallied with Chinook's. And peering down into the gloom below now he realized he could make out scraps of faded cloth upon the lower ledge along with stick-shaped objects that had likely been spears and ceremonial pipes.

Chinook had described the battle here as a war of attrition, with the small force of Shoshone in full command and well able to deny the larger Sioux party entry via the Slot, resulting in a sniping war in which the defenders held every advantage. Other than an escape route, that was. The Shoshone were trapped in the Abyss while the Sioux had totally free range of movement outside yet were unable to penetrate the enemy defences.

How it finished he didn't know and didn't need to. Sufficient for him to know and believe he couldn't enter the eerie basin with the Doubletree killers commanding the pass any more than could the Sioux. And there was supposed to be no other way of infiltrating the basin. Or was there?

'Tell me about the Sioux boys, Younger Bear.'

The young Sioux blinked. 'You know?'

'Only what Chinook told me. He wasn't sure it was true or not. Is it?'

'For God's sake, Duane,' Jesse complained from above, "are you going to tell me what the Sam Hill we're doing here? This place is giving me the jim-jams.'

Duane just nodded to the guide, who made a sign across his chest before speaking.

'Some years ago, in my lifetime, two Indian boys came here hunting, and they climbed down to the bottom to see what they could find of value of the old warriors. This of course was wicked, for this place of death is sacred. But they were punished for their sins when one slipped into this stream and the other tried to save him. They were swept away under the earth and stone.'

'And?'

'When the tribesmen rode round to enter the Abyss by the pass, they found the boys very frightened and bruised, but alive.'

Duane had an odd look on his face as he nodded. 'Good. Glad to hear your version tallies with Chinook's.'

'Just a goddamned minute,' Jesse cut in sharply. 'If you're thinking of trying what a couple of crack-brained kids might've got away with, count me out, bucko. Count out anyone with half a brain for that matter. What's wrong with you anyway, Duane? You're taking this crummy chase like it was life or death. It's just a bunch of lousy drygulchers, for God's sake. They're holed up like rats in there and if they don't die from cold and starvation the law will catch up with them likely sooner than later without amateurs like us getting ourselves killed trying to play Rangers. I'm as sore as you are about what happened. But I don't want to die to prove it. And I damn well won't.'

Duane was climbing back up to the horses. In the full light his brother saw his face was set in exactly the same way he'd seen as a child when he'd set his mind on something and you knew dynamite wouldn't shift him.

'I'm not asking you to do anything,' he said as he untied his roll. 'Except wait down by the Slot with Younger Bear and the horses until I've done whatever needs doing at the caves.'

'So you're going through with it!' Jesse was enraged. 'Pull a suicide stunt. Get killed. And for what?' He flung an arm wildly. 'Just to even scores with a bunch of scum. That's cowboy stuff. We're not vigilantes, we're Eversons.'

Duane had removed his gunbelt. He rolled it up tightly in his weatherproof then lashed the bundle tight with a leather tie.

'You don't get it, Jesse. Sure, I'd like to pay them out if I got the chance. But that's not what I'm after. Those killers were after Dad, and nothing will convince me someone didn't put up money for them to stage that ambush in town. And as long as that, someone remains unidentified then Jordan's life's in danger. So, what option have we got?'

'I sure as hell don't get this, Brother. You come back home because you hear Jordan's sick, you stick your neck out and get shot, knowing someone's out to do for him. Then you turn lawman-possemaster overnight, now you are busting to get yourself killed – all for Jordan. How come? You and him never did hit it off. Never. Why should you kill yourself for him?'

'I'm not doing it for him,' Duane said without looking up.

'Who then?'

'Maybe I'll get to tell you one day.'

Jesse made no reply. He drew back from his brother the way someone might shrink from a stranger or a madman.

Duane was unfazed. Could be he was loco. Driven to take crazy risks by circumstances. But Chinook and the guide had both indicated a possible chink in the armour of the Abyss and he would test it to the hilt.

He traded nods with Younger Bear, tucked his roll beneath his arm and began the climb down.

The rush of water was deafening at the bottom of the pit, which appeared twice as high from this angle. Duane studied the stream rushing away into the tunnel which the waters had hewn through shaley rock over the ages and took a deep shuddering breath. He knew if he delayed he would never do it. A second breath pumped his lungs and he dived headlong and was gone.

Thirty seconds of tumbling terror later found him being spewed out into a rock pond so deep he failed to touch the bottom with his feet when the torrent hammered him down. Frantically he fought his way back up until erupting into daylight with huge black sentinel stones surrounding him. Kicking and sputtering he somehow fought his way across to the bank where he wedged his fingers into a crevice and held on grimly, willing the strength back into his battered body.

He was hurt, dazed, tasted blood in his mouth. At last he managed to haul his battered body out, to sprawl on his back upon solid rock staring upwards at the beetling cliffs.

Maybe Jesse was right, accusing him of being loco, he mused. He must be. But being both crazy and inside the 'impenetrable' Abyss was something he could live with.

Duane froze with one boot six inches off the ground. He didn't breathe, didn't blink. As motionless as a buck caught out of cover unsure if the wolves in the woods have sighted him or not. Before daring to move he must be dead set certain the enemy had not heard him even though he'd just clearly heard them.

It was several hours later, a tense eternity which he'd spent working his infinitely cautious way round the base of the cliffs along the northern side of the great basin. Making eastward all the time. Focused on the caverns overlooking the trail. Headed there.

The wind buffeted him and above the rim lightning jagged across a darkening sky. More rain. He could smell it.

That was the least of his concerns. Were they going to move or speak again, or did their abrupt silence indicate they were aware of him? That maybe right now they could be making their stealthy way around the giant slab of yellow talus which stood on its side in front of the caves, which had provided the cover under which he'd been able to infiltrate so close.

It was a full minute which felt more like an hour before he finally lowered his foot to the lava-buckled floor of the Abyss. The dim sounds, which had

stopped him stone cold, had resumed. The scraping
of metal against stone; maybe somebody scooping
water from the tiny streamlet which cut between the
talus slab and the cave entrance. Then he heard a
horse snort, the murmur of voices, silence again.

He got behind a knob of ancient rock and sleeved
cold sweat from his face. In his mind's eye he was
recalling every detail of this north-eastern corner
here as he'd studied it from the southern rim earlier
in the day, pictured the most likely spot where the
horses might be kept and speculated a look-out
would need to be posted in order to command a
watch over the Slot. He'd figured then, and affirmed
it now, a sentry would have to be positioned off somewhere to his right beyond the bulging granite shoulder which shielded the caves from the entrance.

So he began belly-wriggling left.

The talus slab, whose fall must have set the entire
Abyss trembling, was some fifteen feet high by
double that in length. The left corner loomed close,
and he caught the whiff of something cooking as he
paused to make a last-minute double-check on his
sixguns. He stared at them for a moment, acutely
conscious of how violently his whole life had
changed, how swift and almost unwitting his transi-
tion from horseman to the man behind the gun.

He removed his hat before angling one eye round
the edge of the time-weathered stone.

Before him lay the stream and beyond that an
open space reaching across to the uneven stone
apron which abutted the foot of the caves. There
were five caves in all in this sector, three at ground
level and two more at differing heights above. He
could see where footholes had been hewn into the

living rock, caught a glimpse of a man-made ladder in the larger of the upper caverns where a grease lamp burning dimly threw dancing shadows across ancient walls.

The ground-level caves stood in deepening gloom. In the one furthest to his right, and nearest the granite shoulder, he glimpsed a mule's hindquarters and heard a hoof rattle stone.

He couldn't see the look-out from here but was certain he spied a wisp of smoke drifting from beyond that shoulder.

'Where's my chaw, woman?'

The voice floating down from the lighted cave made him start. He was warning himself to relax when, out of nowhere, a jolt of staghorn lightning stabbed through the dark and drizzling sky to illuminate everything in shimmering blue light. This caused the animals to raise a ruckus which was swallowed without trace by the belated thunderclap which shook the mighty mountains.

It seemed much darker immediately following the flash, and he knew he must take advantage of this. Time wasn't going to make his task any easier, and he'd already figured out his battle plan. The couple above first, then the look-out. It was likely a whole lot riskier than a brown-legged kid fishing for crawfish using his toes for the lure in Red Warrior River. Risk was this game's name.

Fifty yards of deadly open space stretched before him.

He delayed just long enough to fire himself up. These people were the ones who'd murdered Preacher Davis and put Mimsi Peach in Doc Greenlease's four-bed hospital, he reminded himself.

And had come within a whisper of murdering his father.

All he needed.

He was up and snaking forward across no man's land with his heart in his mouth and one Colt .45 in hand. His mind insisted this was just like springing a trap on a bunch of wild mustangs somewhere south of Tucson. But his swift-moving body wasn't fooled for a moment. This was about as dangerous as life could get and he was scared as hell.

But he kept going. Ten paces, twenty-five and nothing happened.

His eyes snapped upwards, expecting the sharp stab of muzzle flash from the lighted cavern any second. He swallowed painfully when the flitting shadow of someone's head and shoulders crossed a wall and was gone.

A final spurt and the darkness of the centre lower cave closed round him. Picking his way through trail junk and saddles, he reached the back wall and immediately began clambering up, using the carved footholds.

Still nothing.

He was having a charmed run.

So far.

Faint light outlined the hole in the floor above, daubing his head and shoulders. He had guns in both hands now as he heaved himself into the gloom of the first high cave and eased across the floor to peer round the corner of the man-made entryway into a chamber where a cookpot sat upon a fire which burned away merrily, lending walls and ceiling a warm, ruddy glow.

The man and woman were squatted cross-legged

on either side of a little camp table eating from tin plates. The scene appeared so normal and domesticated that for a moment he felt almost like an intruder.

Then the man glanced at the fire and with the light fully upon his face Duane recognized him as he'd seen him last, rushing towards the front doors of St Gabriel's with guns in his hairy fists, hell-bent on killing his father.

Cocking the pistols he stepped into the light and growled, 'Reach!'

Everything happened at once.

More like startled feral animals than anything human, the man and woman erupted from the floor to fly in opposite directions, the woman screaming like a banshee, the ugly, ape-like man clawing at his holster as swift as anything Duane had ever seen.

Fingers on triggers, Duane involuntarily hesitated almost a fraction too long, mesmerized by the spine-chilling reality of this situation he'd sought after and forced upon himself. Then the split second of shock was behind him and he was whole again, concentrating fiercely on the frenzied figure of the man reefing up the big black gun, screaming obscenities, beast-like and grotesque.

Duane jerked trigger and the cave exploded with the ear-slamming crack as Monk hurled his agile body sideways.

The bullet ripped through the killer's flank, the impact spinning him violently away towards the lip, as, from the corner of his eye, Duane glimpsed the limber woman seize a dangling length of rope to go swinging out over the ledge.

A long hairy arm shot out at the last moment and

Monk's fingers hooked onto a heavy saddle-bag to try and save himself from falling. Their eyes met and locked as the killer fought to bring his right-hand Colt into play, one pair blazing with insane rage, the other's almost calm as the eye of the cyclone. Duane jerked trigger again. He fired too fast. The slug ricocheted off the stone floor and ripped upwards, taking a chunk of denim, leather and outlaw flesh with it to slam against the roof. Off balance, screaming and in agony, Monk missed his footing again and next instant was tumbling over the drop in a frantic flurry of arms and legs, howling all the long way down.

Duane never moved faster. He was to the mouth in a heartbeat, expecting to see the mangled body directly below. Instead he was greeted by a gunflash flaring up at him, orange and wicked. He weaved to one side then opened up as the staggering outlaw vanished into the cavern beneath.

Whirling, he rushed back through the adjacent cave and hurled himself recklessly through the manhole. Gun thunder shook the lower cave and rock splinters peppered his leg as he came plummeting down, lips skinned back from clenched teeth, searching for a target.

He struck, rolled – and ducked wildly.

'Dirty, stinkin' lawdog son of a bitch!'

Monk was coming at him, a shambling silhouette against the lighter hue of the talus. He was triggering furiously but there was no accuracy in his gunwork. Blood was spilling from his cracked head and he was plainly out on his feet, with only pain, rage and murderous instinct keeping him in it.

But a wild or lucky shot could kill a man just as dead as any other.

Sprawled on the stone with slugs air-whipping all about him, Duane had a shaved splinter of time to make a truly desperate decision. He couldn't miss at this range. He could shoot the man down, or he could try taking him alive and getting him back to Doubletree where he might prove to be the only man with all the answers to the things he must know.

He was up.

The killer was so close he could smell the rank stink of him, imagined he felt the heat of his rage coming off him. Yet he was weaving like a drunk while icy intent propelled Rider towards him. Duane drew back his gun arm then swung with the full weight of his body behind the terrible blow. It exploded against the side of Monk's bloodied head and he went down as if pole-axed.

Suddenly spent, Duane lurched backwards until supported by the wall. Shaking sweat out of his eyes and with lungs rasping like bellows, he was forced to wait until the big ganglion of nerves in his belly quit trembling violently. Only then did he fumble for bullets in his shell-belt and laboriously thumbed them into the smoking chambers.

He felt like the survivor of a war, but this one wasn't over yet.

Far from it, maybe.

'Monk! He's killed Monk!' The cry came from far out in the darkness. The woman's voice. She sounded hysterical. Her cry went unanswered. Then she shouted again. 'The third cave, Ringo!'

'I've got him, Zara!'

The man's voice sounded so close it sent Duane diving for the floor. It must be the look-out and he'd come in faster than Duane would have thought possible.

Sprawled motionless in the dark with death stalking close, Duane was acutely aware of his body; the beating of his heart; the blood pounding in his ears. Every tense muscle in his lean body vibrated violently before it relaxed, then, miraculously, relaxed completely.

He realized with sudden crystal clarity that the transformation had taken place. He'd pursued the killers as an ordinary man forced to do something against his nature. Now he was no longer that man, but felt closer to the men he hunted. The crucible of danger had tempered and hardened him beyond belief, and he was without fear or uncertainty as he rolled over and stalked towards the dim outline of the cavern mouth.

Next instant the interior was again shattered by the bellow of gun thunder and the chamber was filled with flying lead. Throwing himself full length, Duane realized Ringo had appeared at a man-made hole in the wall away from the mouth, saw his contorted face illuminated by the hellish gunflashes as he continued the barrage.

Duane fired once and the guns fell silent. He heard a low cry, then staggering steps before he glimpsed the buckled-over figure lurching out onto the apron, holding his guts in with both hands. Duane was raising his smoking cutter again when the outlaw moaned in total agony and fell full length. He lay on his back with one boot stuttering against stone. He tried to speak, to cry out, but choked on blood.

'Ringo!'

Duane's eyes stabbed the gloom, eventually detected the white of the woman's shirt showing behind the brush thicket he'd passed coming in. He reloaded with steady fingers and started in triggering. He was shooting to miss but she didn't know that. And when one of his slugs whispered too close – knowing Flowers to be dead and Monk badly injured, perhaps dead also – Zara's steely nerve failed at last.

Slowly Duane lowered his guns at the sound of running boot-heels fading far out beyond the talus.

There was a bad moment when he looked out to see no sign of Monk's body below the caves. Then he detected the trail of slime and blood like the track of a broken-backed snail upon the stone and followed it across to the ice stream to where the crumpled figure lay against a basalt rock .

Somehow the man named Monk had hauled his battered body that far before collapsing.

He stood above him with a Colt .45 in either hand to see what the fall had done. The desperado killer who'd tried to murder his father looked like something you'd find on a slab in the morgue. Cursing softly, fearing he might be left with nobody who could answer all the questions clamouring for clarification, he dropped on one knee at the man's side.

Monk was motionless, battered, broken and bloodied from head to toe. He did not seem to breathe. Yet when Duane placed the flat of his hand over his rotten heart he felt it thudding as smoothly as a big Swiss clock.

And the quiet man from Alameda smiled like a wolf. He would live. And while ever a man lived he could talk.

*

'Sorry, Mr Tyran,' said the yard hand posted at the barn door. 'No admittance, not today.'

The boy's pale face flushed.

'What the hell do you mean, Jackson? I can go any place I please any goddamn time. Step aside right now or you can kiss your job goodbye.'

'Please, Ty,' his sister said anxiously, the wind blowing down off the high country tossing her blonde curls about her lovely face. 'Jesse said this is private business, and Duane supported him.'

'I don't give a damn, Sis. This is my place more than it is theirs. They can't just ride in here with some shot-up stranger, drag him off to the barn, then tell everyone to keep out. I'm going to tell Dad.'

He stormed away, the girl running after him. Across at the mansion, the figures of Jordan Everson, a clutch of ranch hands and bodyguards and the always sober-faced Mrs Barker could be seen staring across the wind-blowing yard towards them.

Nobody on Cloud Valley seemed to know what was going on, and this was a situation his father would not tolerate, his youngest son was quite sure. He beckoned but Jordan didn't move. He was sicker than ever today, and looked it. For reasons nobody could understand, the normally composed housekeeper looked pale as a ghost; had done ever since Cloud Valley's blustery early morning had been interrupted by the arrival of four travel-stained riders on played-out horses: a young Indian, Jesse and Duane accompanied by an evil-looking man with strapping around his ugly head and one leg, and both hands tied behind his back.

Monk Hendry was still sitting his saddle at that moment – almost.

He was astride his horse but the rope knotted cruelly under his left ear, the end slung over a rafter high in the upper gloom of the barn roof, was now so tight that his backside was lifted a full quarter inch out of the leather.

Great beads of sweat coursed down over his battered features and three expressionless faces stared up at him from the floor.

'Again,' Duane said quietly.

The rope's end was secured around the barrel of a hand-winch. Jesse gave the handle a quarter turn and a strangled gasp of fear was torn from the killer's lips as he was raised a fraction higher. He was using his powerful thighs, pressing hard against the horse's withers, to refract some of the terrible pressure on his neck. But his vision was going now, and worse, he knew they would go through with it. Commit cold-blooded murder. The bastards! They must think being Everson's sons they could get away with it. And maybe they could at that.

'All right – all right damn your stinkin' souls to hell – I'll tell you. Let me down!'

'That's not the way it's done,' Duane said coldly. 'Name first, then you get to breathe again.'

Monk's eyes were bulging from their sockets, his big frog mouth gasping for air. Then Jesse leaned a hand on the taut rope and the extra pressure seemed to squeeze the words past his lips;

'Leonard, you miserable sons of bitches. Gray Leonard. He paid me five hundred to put your old man in the box!'

They were lowering him to the floor, still choking

to breathe, when the barn doors burst inward and Jordan came storming in trailed by four bodyguards, Tyran and Beth. The spectacle of the bound man with the rope still round his neck, flopping and flipping in the straw like a fish out of water with the brothers standing over him even rendered Jordan speechless, maybe for the first time anyone could remember.

Although Monk Hendry did not know it all, he knew enough to satisfy his audience. And with his hands freed at last, a desperately needed whiskey in his fist and Jesse's gun muzzle resting against the back of his ugly neck, he sang like a bird. The brothers had outtoughed the tough desperado, and whether they would have hanged him in their father's barn or were simply bluffing was something he would never know in whatever short slice of life he might have ahead.

'We hit the bottle the day he hired me,' he began, surrounded by a sea of faces in the great front room. 'I told him I never took a job unless I knew the whole set-up, so he had no choice but to talk up. And so he did.'

He paused to blink painfully across at Jordan.

'Seemed you was just too big, too rich and too blamed greedy for Leonard. Told me he could be as big as you if you hadn't blocked his every move. Told me straight out he'd been tryin' for some time to take you out.' He half grinned. 'Seemed he hired some local nobodies to take pot-shots at you, but they weren't up to the job. Even tried to jump your hardcase son here over in the canyon, so one of 'em did, but they screwed that up too. It was around then that Leonard realized he needed a pro like me, but I

guess he'd still be fiddle-faddlin' about it only for the
skirt. That's what really fired him up in the end. The
skirt. Said you can no more miss out on a good roll
in the hay than you can pass up stitchin' up a
hundred thousand dollar deal—'

'A woman?' Duane cut in. 'What woman?'

'He means Clarissa Harte,' Jordan growled from
his deep chair, his seamed face pale and sick. 'She
was seeing Leonard but I took her away from him.
So, vermin, you agreed to murder me for five
hundred dollars. Is that what you're saying?'

Monk's simian head bobbed. He was too far gone
for defiance. He wanted a doctor, some care, someplace to rest up; all the things his captors had denied
him throughout the punishing ride back from the
Abyss. He hurt all over and the hangman was waiting.
He could barely muster a resentful glitter from red-
rimmed eyes as he fixed his stare on Duane, yet at the
same time, seemed deeply puzzled.

'How come you got to be so hard, Everson? You're
a rich man's kid. Where'd you learn to read sign and
throw lead and cut up rough? We'd have all been
home free but for you . . . one spoon-fed silvertail
playin' bounty hunter—'

' Your head's scrambled, scum.' Jordan nodded at
his eldest son. It was Jesse who brought you down,
not Duane.'

'I know who done for me—' Monk began but
Duane cut him off sharply.

'Of course it was Jesse,' he stated, shooting the
killer a warning look. That was how he'd insisted the
story be told; that was how it would be. Then, 'All
right, we know enough for now.' He nodded to his
father. 'We'll take him in. Ready, Jesse?'

'Sure.'

Jesse Everson looked the part in the role he'd always played so well as he housed his revolver, seized Monk by the shoulder and reefed him to his feet. This was the Jesse whom Cloud Valley had always known, assured, commanding, the man born to call the shots and do it with style.

Only Jordan looked deeply thoughtful as he trailed them out onto the gallery. But his attention was diverted when he noticed the speck of receding movement a mile or so along the town trail. He turned, curious, to a yardman on the steps.

'Whose rig is that down yonder?'

'Mrs Barker, boss. She lit out in one almighty hurry so soon as y'all went indoors. Seemed mighty flustered about somethin' which sure ain't like that woman at all, so I'm thinkin'.'

'Curious,' Jordan frowned at his sons. 'What do you make of that?'

The brothers shrugged and went to the hitch rail. They were haggard and spent but not yet done. As they heaved the outlaw into his saddle before mounting up together, Duane glanced about and seemed to sense that the cloud that had hung over the spread ever since his return was already lifting. It was only too bad, he thought as they rode off to a ragged cheer from the gallery, that their getting to the root of one threat to Jordan's life gave them no power over the other. He was still a very sick man. By the look of him his father would be lucky to last another month.

Nobody seemed to notice Tyran and Beth staring at one another in pale-faced silence as the riders clattered from the yard.

10

Ride the Wind South

The valise was now almost filled with fat packets of high denomination banknotes, securities and share certificates. The teller, who was doing such an efficient job of packing the glossy leather bag with the embossed initials G.L. on the flap, now returned from the main room of the Montana and Western Bank building empty-handed and smiling.

'That's everything, Mr Leonard—'

He broke off as Leonard snatched up the valise and shoved him roughly aside in his haste to leave. As the gambler burst into the ante-room where the manager was engaged in conversation with a female clerk at a corner desk, Mrs Barker turned sharply from the window, her face white and angry.

'What kept you so long, you fool?' she hissed as they hurried for the stairs. 'You said it would only take five minutes.'

'It took five years to acquire this,' he panted, slapping the valise as they reached the ground floor passageway leading to the rear entrance. 'And who knows when if ever I'd be free to come back here for anything I might leave behind . . .' Leonard's voice trailed off as his steps slowed. He stood staring at the glass door. 'Where . . . where's Turk?'

The woman's hand flew to her lips. They'd arrived at the Western with four men from the Domino. Four reliable doormen. There was now not one to be seen. Impulsively she rushed to the door and jerked it open. Rearing backwards, Leonard darted a hand for an inside pocket as he glimpsed grim-jawed Sheriff Buck Tune coming through. But there was closer danger as he realized when two grimed and stubbled men whom he didn't recognize at first glance emerged from the utilities room to cover him with cocked Colt .45s.

Leonard's right hand froze before it could touch gun handle. Jesse Everson rested his gun muzzle against his temple with one hand while the other reached in and relieved the gambler of the ace in the hole he never got to use.

Ashen-faced and disbelieving, Leonard stared into Jesse's blue eyes and saw his fate writ large there a moment before the vicious backhander whipped across his face and felled him to the floor.

'That'll do, Jesse,' Duane said in his quiet way. Then he seized the dazed man by the lapels, hauled him across the floor and backed him up against the wall. 'You won't need any roughing up to make you talk, will you, cardsharp? Not when you know we've not only got Hendry in the cells singing his heart out, but also that fine map of St Gabriel's you sketched for him . . . with the names of everything in your handwriting, you won't. Isn't that so, you murdering bastard?'

The sheriff approached holding the housekeeper by the arm. As yet he had nothing positive against Mrs Barker other than that she had fled Cloud Valley and alerted the gambler to his danger, then accompanied him to the bank. At this stage that was more than enough circumstantial evidence to warrant her arrest.

The woman appeared dazed. Gray Leonard was a man totally destroyed in moments, yet he managed somehow to maintain a veneer of composure as the brothers took it in turns to list each damaging charge Monk Hendry had laid against him. It wasn't until Duane finally mentioned Clarissa Harte that the gambler came apart like something made of wet straw.

'Your precious, stinking, grab-all old man!' he almost sobbed. 'Owns everything, won't let anyone share anything, just takes and takes and takes. The only reason that son of a bitch took an interest in Clarissa was because he knew I was in love with her. So he stole her, just like that. And that was the day I made up my mind to get rid of him any way I could. And if it weren't for tenth-raters who couldn't shoot straight and poison that didn't work, I'd have s—'

'Gray, don't, for God's sake be quiet!' the woman implored desperately, but he dismissed her with a snarl. Gray Leonard was a realist. He knew he was doomed and damned, that Monk had slung the noose around his throat. But he would have his say. It was all he had left.

'She was too damned cautious, and my lackeys couldn't shoot straight,' he confessed bitterly, as though acknowledging the hopelessness of his guilt and not giving a damn whom he brought down with him now.

The woman began to weep. Gray Leonard jabbed a finger at her.

'Another Jordan victim!' he said as three men with guns listened wide-eyed. It was as though he had to blacken Jordan Everson before life, death or justice might silence his tongue forever. The man was way out of control and tears ran down his cheeks as he continued to rant and rage, as though compelled to shock while he still had the power to do so, before they silenced him. To shock, and perhaps to boast at just how clever and almost successful he'd been.

'Yeah, that's right, your wonderful daddy was rolling in the hay with the housekeeper out there in between girlfriends. Telling her he loved her and would marry her one day. She believed him, the damned fool. But his carry-on with Clarissa was the last straw for Janet as it was for me. We go back quite a ways, her and me. So when she came griping to me about Everson I saw an opportunity and made her a proposition. Her husband operates an apothecary's and she wanted to get square. Tyran was in hock to me over his eyeballs, so the kid and Janet here worked on Jordan to get rid of Doc Greenlease. Soon as he was out of the picture we went to work on the medication he was taking for the gout – adding just a smidgen more of arsenic to his medicine every day.'

He paused to sneer at the weeping woman.

'And that's all he got, thanks to you,' he said contemptuously. 'Sick but not dead. If you'd done your job right he'd be long gone and I would never have had to fall back on a Judas scum like Monk Hendry . . .'

His tirade cut off in mid sentence. It was as though the frenzied outburst had husked him out, leaving him empty and staring into the awful reality of what lay ahead. Slobber dripped off his chin as he stared at the Eversons as though they were total strangers. The woman cursed and tried to rake his face with her nails. But the sheriff got between them and led the former conspirators outside where his deputies were waiting, the shuffling gambling king offering no resistance.

They left behind two other utterly exhausted 'old men' who hoped to feel young again someday as they trudged heavily through the bank to head for the Deacon Bench and saloon-keeper Dockerty's elixir of life.

Sunlight shimmered on the lake.

Duane led Joker around the water's edge to help the horse walk the weariness out of its muscles. He smoked and Jesse talked, just like the old days. Only real difference was that, in those far off times, Jesse would likely have been bragging it up whereas today he was as serious as a man could be.

'You're quitting, aren't you, Duane?'

Duane didn't deny it.

Jesse's eyes were on the mansion. 'You're quitting and you plan on leaving me here the way you did once before. That's why you lied to the old man about what happened in the high country. You built me up so that both him and I would want me to to stay on, so don't try and deny it. But I can't do it, Brother. Jordan's old and ready to hand over the reins but I'm not the man to take over. Maybe once I was, not now. You saw that plain in the high country. I still talk a good fight but that's about where it ends.'

'What happened to you, Jesse? You always had grit to spare. What'd they do to you in Wyoming?'

They stopped for Joker to crop the good grass. Doc Greenlease's rig was still in the yard. Jordan had grudgingly invited him out and the medico had already grumpily run some tests to confirm that he'd been on an arsenic diet, but would recover. Jana had not accompanied Greenlease out but Duane had ridden into town and spent a night with her he'd never forget. Tyran was in deep trouble with his father over his gambling debts and associated matters, but likely could count himself lucky it wasn't far worse.

'Not what anyone did to me,' Jesse said after a thoughtful silence. 'More like what I did to me.' A shrug. 'Too many women, too much whiskey, too much yearning for the good old days here, I guess. Who knows?'

'So, why'd you come back?'

Jesse laughed. 'Hell! You think I'd want to miss all this hooraw and excitement?'

'We did something special here, Bro,' Duane said in his serious way. 'We worked together just like old times and we saved Jordan's life and put some people behind bars who—'

'You did a big thing,' Jesse corrected roughly, tugging out his cigars. 'Let's not crap on any more than we have to, Rider. I did a lot of showing off then folded like a crooked deck the moment the going got tough, but you saw it through. Risked your life a dozen times and came out trumps. We both know it, so why try and dress it up as something it wasn't? I'm not ashamed to be called yellow.'

That was a huge admission coming from this man.

'Remember the Blue Hole rustlers, Jesse? Back in seventy-one, we were just kids, but we ran that bunch down and you saved my life when they ambushed us on Catlow Ridge. You stood against four of them and put two in the ground, looking out for me. It was the bravest thing I ever saw.'

'Ancient history.'

They stopped at the jetty. Jordan's sailboat was tied up to the pier. It was blue and white. A cormorant sat on a spar. Joker gave the bird his evil eye. The black didn't like birds, most other horses, or cold-climate country. Duane was with him only on the last. The South was in his blood. It was this thought which kept him focused on what he wanted to achieve before returning to the house.

'Jesse, you admit you've just been killing time in Wyoming. But can't you see how things are here now? You've got everything a man could ever want. Forget that buffalo dust about what happened in the mountains. You went further than the rest of the posse, including Tune himself, so just remember that. But chasing badmen isn't what ranching is about. Jordan's ready to take a back seat, he thinks the sun shines out of you, you're a hero to the whole county and all you have to do is tell me you'll take over so I can get back home where I belong. And here's the sweetener, if you need one. You can have my share of Cloud Valley, if I've still got one. I'll tell the old man. I've got all I want in Arizona. What do you say?'

Jesse was staring into the distance. 'It's too long since we hunted those rustlers, Brother.' He shook his golden head. 'It'd take guts to stand up to Jordan and carry the full load on my shoulders. Guts . . . and character, I guess. I just don't have enough of either any more.'

They stood together in the taut silence as a minute that could have been a chunk of eternity went by. Each man busy with his own thoughts, Duane staggered by where his seemed to be leading him.

'OK,' he said casually as they started for the house. 'But Tune wants me in town this afternoon to help draft the formal charges. Last night was too much a cattle-call at the Deacon once the word got around what we'd been up to. How about meeting me at the Harmonica for chow around six? Just the two of us.'

Jesse's magical smile flashed white. 'Six it is. Hey, there's the old man beckoning from the back porch. Five'll get you ten he wants to tell us how he always figured it was Leonard behind all his troubles, and that he never really trusted that housekeeper.'

'No bet,' Duane grinned. But the smile didn't touch his eyes.

The den looked bright and less cluttered now. No flowers. Janice Barker had filled the mansion with them to smother the almond whiff of arsenic. Jesse had gone down to the yards to join the men and they were alone in the silence, father and son.

Then abruptly: 'I don't want you to leave again, boy.'

Duane stared. 'What?'

Jordan moved to the windows. He was already looking healthier, moving more freely.

'I'm not used to asking favours, so I'll make it quick. I want you to stay on and boss Cloud Valley. I'll step aside, probably marry Clarissa and move into town and leave you with a clear run. If you want I'll put the place in your name and take care of your brothers and sister financially. What do you say?'

For a long slow moment, Rider Duane couldn't say anything. He was stunned.

Eventually he cleared his throat and adopted a level tone. 'You know I've got to go back. But surely you're talking to the wrong man? Jesse's hand-made for the top-dog job. You're so alike it's as if you were both shelled from the same pod. He can do anything, everybody loves him . . . and if you needed any extra proof, just look what he did in the mountains.'

Jordan turned to face him.

'I know what he did in the mountains. I talked to Younger Bear before he left. I knew you lied.' He almost smiled. 'Damned stupid thing to do, but I admire you for it. And it confirms what I've long half-suspected about you boys. I love your brother, but he's gone soft – all that easy living. But you are hard and strong, Duane. The Valley deserves you and you deserve the Valley.'

'It'd never work,' Duane stated flatly. 'You and me, that is. We were always too different. There's too much bad-blood baggage between us going right back almost to Day One.'

'But you came back, boy. Surely that proves something? It does to me.'

'Not really. Only for Ma I would never have showed.'

'But she's gone twenty years. I don't understand.'

'Ma loved you. I don't know why, but she did. And because she loved you, I had to come back to look out for you. Don't you see? I did all this for her, not you. For Ma! Savvy?'

These were hard words delivered forcefully. The rancher hung his grey head a moment, then nodded.

'You always did talk straight ... too straight mostly.' He raised his head and Duane would never forget the look in his eyes when he said simply, 'I really loved your mother too, you know.'

It was an astonishing admission from this arrogant man. Without precedent. It jolted Duane to his bootstraps, yet warmed him in a way he would not have thought possible. Plainly a lifetime's years of mistrust and misunderstanding could not be erased by a few words; he knew that, yet he still felt they'd journeyed a vast distance in just a few minutes.

'I know you mean that,' he said, reaching for his hat.

'I do. I always meant it. I'm just not always that clever at saying what I feel. But you're still leaving, aren't you?'

'So long, Dad.'

Jordan blinked. 'You haven't called me that in twenty years.'

'It won't be so long until next time you hear it. I promise.'

'You'll be heading south?'

'Must.' He turned for the door, emotion hammering his chest. 'But you have Jesse. He'll stick.'

'No he won't. Would have once, but not now. I'll be alone.'

'No. One way or another, you won't be alone,' he insisted.

He stepped outside, fitting hat to head, astonished and exhilarated, yet at the same time awed by what he knew he must do.

*

Midnight in Doubletree.

Standing by the window of the gloomy upstairs corridor of Plains Hotel, Rider Duane watched a hunting owl fly past the moon and listened to the muffled laughter and voices seeping over the transom of Room 15.

He'd been there an hour and was destined to be there a half-hour later, dragging on his third cigarette, when the dishevelled, giggling girl emerged, paused to chuck him under the chin and say, 'That no-account brother doesn't deserve a faithful watchdog like you, Duane baby,' before making her weaving way off for the staircase, singing snatches of some beer-hall ballad seriously off key.

He waited some more.

The moon had slipped further down the night sky when he eased the door open and entered the room.

Jesse lay sprawled on the bed, sound asleep, drunk and happy. He stood by the bedside studying the handsome face which looked so much younger and more innocent in repose. Then he reached out and, from the gunrig hanging over the bedpost, drew out the long-barrelled Colt .45.

For a long slow time he didn't seem to move or even breathe as he stared down at the gun in his hands.

The girl was pretty and she was interested. Yet he kept glancing up at Dockerty's handsome wall clock above the painting of Washington at Valley Forge. It was gone ten and he'd arranged to meet Duane here at nine. Where the hell was he? And why had he insisted they meet up so early in the morning after their big night anyway? And now he came to think about it, why had his brother insisted they have another big night in town so soon after their last visit anyway? He wanted to believe it had nothing to do with any decision Duane might have made about leaving. With things panning out so well now, Jesse Everson was content to stay on indefinitely. But only if his brother stayed too. They seemed closer than ever these days, and he needed that.

She began running fingers through his thick yellow hair and he was brushing her hand away impatiently when the naked skull and pudgy frame of Dockerty loomed up to the table.

'Your brother wants to see you in my office, Jesse,' the saloonkeeper grunted, jerking his thumb. 'Pronto, he said.'

He didn't waste any time snatching up his hat and heading in back, an annoyed frown cutting his dark brows. The door to the office was open so he walked straight in. The door clicked shut behind him and he whirled to find his brother standing there with hands on hips staring at him so coldly it caused his neck hair to lift. He looked like a stranger.

'What?' he said. 'What's wrong with you? What's going on?'

Duane moved past him and hauled a chair out from under the desk.

'Take a seat and listen. You'd better listen real good.'

Nobody told tall Jesse what to do. But because this was Duane, he swallowed his anger and sat. As Duane

moved past him to come round the table, he noticed
something odd. His brother's holster was empty, but
glancing round he spotted the familiar walnut butt
jutting over the top of the bureau in the far corner.
He looked a question at him but Duane was already
speaking.

'You're hungover again, brother. You never used
to be such a drunk.'

'What?'

'You've changed. But lots of things have changed,
as Jordan and I agreed yesterday. You see we had this
long talk. He wanted me to stay on and take over the
Valley even though you're the elder. I turned him
down, told him I'm leaving for the South tomorrow.'

'Damn it all, man—'

'Told him you'd take over.'

Jesse flushed. 'The hell I am. I told you just yesterday I'm not even staying on if you—'

'He needs you,' Duane cut in brusquely. 'Not me.
You two are the same. I was Ma and you were him.
You and Jordan talk the same language and believe
in the same things. You were born to take over the
spread one day.'

The anger and puzzlement drained from Jesse's
face as he slumped in the chair.

Suddenly he looked old – old and weak.

'You are dropping your bucket down a dry well,
Duane. Judas, man, you saw what happened in the
mountains. I folded just as soon as the going got
tough. That's what I do now. Whatever I might have
had once is long gone. Like I say, I talk a real good
fight, but once a fight turns serious, I'm gone. I could-
n't run Dockerty's joint, much less Cloud Valley.'

'You've lived too easy, too long,' Duane said,

circling the table and fingering his empty holster. 'But you're still an Everson, and you're still going to stay on and take over. Not only that but you'll be the man Jordan wants you to be.'

Jesse leapt to his feet, white with anger.

'Are you loco? Why are you acting so crazy?' He smashed the desk with his fist. 'I'm doing nothing I don't want to do, boy. Not now, not ever.'

It was as if Duane didn't hear.

'You've got no choice.'

'What?'

'Jesse, you were something once. I mean really something. And you can be again, I know it. A man doesn't lose his backbone, just misplaces it sometime. I know this, but before you leave this room you're going to have to prove to me I'm right. I've got to be certain sure about you and the spread before I go, and there's only one sure way I know how to prove it.'

'What the Sam Hill are you mouthing about?'

Duane stepped back from the desk, a cold eyed total stranger. 'Dad deserves a man out there and I mean to give him one. Either that, or he'll lose a son.'

'I'm going!'

'Stay put!' Duane's voice cut. He jerked his chin at the bureau. 'My shooter is over there, you're wearing yours. If you don't measure up, find your backbone and get to do what I want, you're no blind bit of use to me, Brother. And you are going to find your nerve and get to be what you used to be right now, or you'll be dead. Understand what I'm saying? I'm giving you a head start, Jesse. I'm going to that bureau to get my Colt. If I get my hand on it before you shoot then I'll

sure as hell shoot you as I'll know you're no use to
yourself or anybody else. That's how bad I want to go
home. I can't leave Jordan with a loser . . . only with
a man. So make up your mind, mister, I'm on my
way.'

It was the most bizarre moment of Jesse Everson's
life as he realized he was in a ten by ten room with a
raving madman. He shot a desperate glance at the
door. Too late. Duane was almost to the bureau.
Sweat burst out on his forehead and he trembled,
cursed, made to speak but his brother was reaching
for that Colt handle.

'You bastard!' he almost screamed, whipping his
sixgun from leather. 'Die then, if that's what you
want!'

He triggered and the gun went: *click, click, click*.

Disbelievingly, he stared down at it. Then his eyes
jerked up to see Duane leaning against the bureau
empty-handed with a big proud smile on his face.

'Knew you still had it in you, Jesse. A thoroughbred's always a thoroughbred, you know.'

For a timeless moment nothing happened. Then
came the explosion. With a snarl of pure rage, Jesse
Everson charged. Duane was expecting something
but nothing this violent. He felt himself smashed
into the bureau, ducked under one whistling fist but
took the full force of a left rip square in the guts. He
doubled and hung on. They wrestled round the
room doing considerable damage to Dockerty's
furnishings, Jesse cursing and Duane trying to
placate him.

It wasn't until the saloonman burst into the room
screaming obscenities and hollering for his bouncers
that Jesse's attack began to lose momentum. Then

two outsized waiters came storming in, reefed them apart and Dockerty banged his Derringer on his desk for silence.

Fifty dollars apiece lighter on the hip, and Jesse's righteous wrath finally quelled by an over-wordy Dockerty lecture on brotherly love, the brothers quit and went back to the barroom, where Duane spent a good ten minutes trying to persuade Jesse to allow him to buy him at least one drink in order that he might explain.

Jesse wouldn't drink, but at least he listened. He was still mad when he heard how Duane had emptied his Colt overnight in order that nobody would get hurt, but seemed to be cooling down some as he went on to explain exactly what he'd done, and why.

It was his belief that Jesse had to be forced into what he thought was a life and death situation before he could prove to himself that he was not the washed-up bum he'd come to believe. Duane conceded it was desperate medicine, but exulted that it had worked. For if Jesse hadn't been afraid to duel to the death with him, how could the good life on the Valley intimidate him?

His reward was seeing the full impact of what had happened begin to dawn in his brother's eyes. Life had dragged the man down but he had been saved.

The light was rekindled. He believed in himself again. He was redeemed.

'So long, Dad.'

'I still wish you wouldn't go, Duane.'

'I'll be back. And it won't be another eight years before I see you either.'

'You're damned right it won't.' Jordan laughed

with some of his old booming volume. 'Right, honey?'

Clarissa crossed the room and took Jordan's hand.

'We're getting married mid summer, Duane.' She smiled. 'Your father, I mean we . . . are honeymooning down south and wondered if. . . .'

'If I'd like you to visit with me on the ranch?' He finished for her. 'It's a date. And best of luck to you both, Dad. . . .'

They shook hands for the first time in memory.

'Incidentally, son,' Jordan said as they went outside to see Jesse go galloping by bawling orders to a loafing hand, 'about the horses. You might as well know I switched from beef to horses, hoping that might draw you back. Who knows? Maybe they helped.'

'Maybe they did. . . .'

Soon Joker was carrying him beneath the title gate with the figures grouped before the house receding into the morning haze. With just a couple of things to finalize in town he would soon be on his way home. The long, yearned-for, journey home.

He'd made his good-byes, or at least those few he'd dared make. The trail beckoned and Joker stamped impatiently to be gone as he put the finishing touches to the saddling. And yet he delayed, standing by the horse's head to stare off uncertainly along Placer's false-fronted canyon.

The irony of this moment was not lost on Rider Duane. He'd been forced to dig deep and dredge up courage he'd never known he possessed over the past weeks, then he'd played a dangerous hand in helping his brother recover his. Yet right at the finale of his Montana odyssey his own nerve had failed him. Totally. He'd farewelled everyone but the one who really counted, and fear was the reason. Whether it was fear of rejection or fear of surrendering his precious freedom, he couldn't be sure. He only hoped she might understand somehow, wouldn't hate him too much for being such a coward.

Joker had had enough of this. The horse jerked his sooty head around to fake a snap at him with big teeth.

'OK, OK, we're going.'

He swung up and a couple of earlybirds across the street from the livery called and waved. He didn't return the greeting. He was supposed to be feeling great yet he'd seldom felt worse. He deliberately kicked the horse who grunted in surprise and started off to swing round the corner where Placer Street met the south trail.

''Allo, Rider.'

He jerked hard on the reins and twisted in the saddle. She stood on the plankwalk before the saloon in the early morning light, holding her hair back off her face in the breeze, just smiling at him as it seemed she had been doing all his life, as though her being here at this hour was the most natural thing in the world.

And maybe it was.

He turned his face to the way ahead. Joker started acting up but went still at a soft word. Duane's eyes were on the distances with a faraway look that slowly gave way to his rare smile.

He slipped his boot from stirrup, glanced over his shoulder. The girl stared at him disbelievingly, not daring to move until he patted Joker's sooty black back. Then she seemed to fly rather than run, swinging up behind effortlessly as only she could to wrap her arms tightly about him and press her laughing face against his back.

They rode on out, and the wind was blowing warmer from the South.